W9-AJH-367

A PLAY-BASED, READING PROGRAM
FOR EMERGING READERS AND
AN ESSENTIAL READING CURRICULUM FOR CAREGIVERS

CAROLINE WILCOX UGURLU, PH.D.

Letters are Characters
A Play-Based, Reading Program for Emerging Readers and an Essential Reading Curriculum for Caregivers
All Rights Reserved.
Copyright © 2019 Caroline Wilcox Ugurlu, Ph.D.
v6.0

The opinions expressed in this manuscript are solely the opinions of the author and do not represent the opinions or thoughts of the publisher. The author has represented and warranted full ownership and/or legal right to publish all the materials in this book.

This book may not be reproduced, transmitted, or stored in whole or in part by any means, including graphic, electronic, or mechanical without the express written consent of the publisher except in the case of brief quotations embodied in critical articles and reviews.

Outskirts Press, Inc.
http://www.outskirtspress.com

ISBN: 978-1-9772-0679-4

Illustrations by Caroline Wilcox Ugurlu, Ph.D. Author Photo © 2019 Terry Augustyn, Nutmeg Photography. All rights reserved – used with permission.

Outskirts Press and the "OP" logo are trademarks belonging to Outskirts Press, Inc.

PRINTED IN THE UNITED STATES OF AMERICA

Dedication

For AJ, who breathed imagination into every part of this book
For Samantha, who added color and song
For my husband, who made it all possible
For everyone who gave encouragement along the way during this four-year project
For little readers, especially the ones who struggle,
I want to hold your hand and tell you I understand
And for upstanders,
Who show the world how to care

Parents are children's first and most important teachers,
and reading is a child's first and most important subject.

For children ages 4–7

Trying to Read

Once there was a very young child who loved stories, characters, and books.
He understood them deeply, and in his heart each message he took.
When it came time to read, he could not wait to learn,
For to read on his own was the thing for which he most yearned.

But the letters and their sounds in his brain just didn't stick.
Teachers and other kids whispered that he wasn't very quick.
"Work harder," they said, and he went off sadly to hide,
Burying his disappointment and fear deep inside.

He cried many tears at the young age of six;
He felt lost and alone with a problem he couldn't fix.
Then along came someone who understood his mind,
Who taught him so he could learn and always was kind.

Sadly those who could not see his struggle and made him feel small
Had not studied or done their homework, no, not at all.
If they had, they would have known how to better teach
This boy who struggled, was heartsick, and so out of reach.

For those who when trying to read have been made to feel shame,
Know that it is not you who are to blame.
There is an army of reading angels trying to make it right,
To teach the world that nearly everyone can learn to read with delight.

Join them if you will by reading this book and spreading its message.

Table of Contents

Introduction

We are facing a reading crisis in the United States that has profound effects. Valid and reliable research from universities, government agencies, and independent firms unambiguously confirms that the majority of children are not learning to read fluently and deeply (see references). This has devastating effects on our children, our communities, and our world. Together we can make a course correction. We know how to help struggling readers so they don't have to hide and feel diminished. And we know how to make nearly everyone read to their highest potential. So let us not waste any time. Let's do this together.

The goal of this book is to provide essential information for you, the parents/caregivers, while at the same time giving you the tools to help your children break the phonemic code (understanding letter to sound relationships). Cracking the phonemic code is the first step to successful reading. Here is how to get started:

1. Read the parent/guardian page first. (You will find a page for you after every three letters to give you time to absorb the information.) There is some repetition on these pages, and this is intentional. We all learn best through repetition.
2. Plan daily special time with your child to "play with letter characters." Start the time with the "Letters, letters, play with me; letters, letters, A, B, C…" song. There is a suggested melody, or you can set it to a tune that your child loves. Skywrite the letters with your index finger when you say them in the song. Here is a suggested tune that works well:

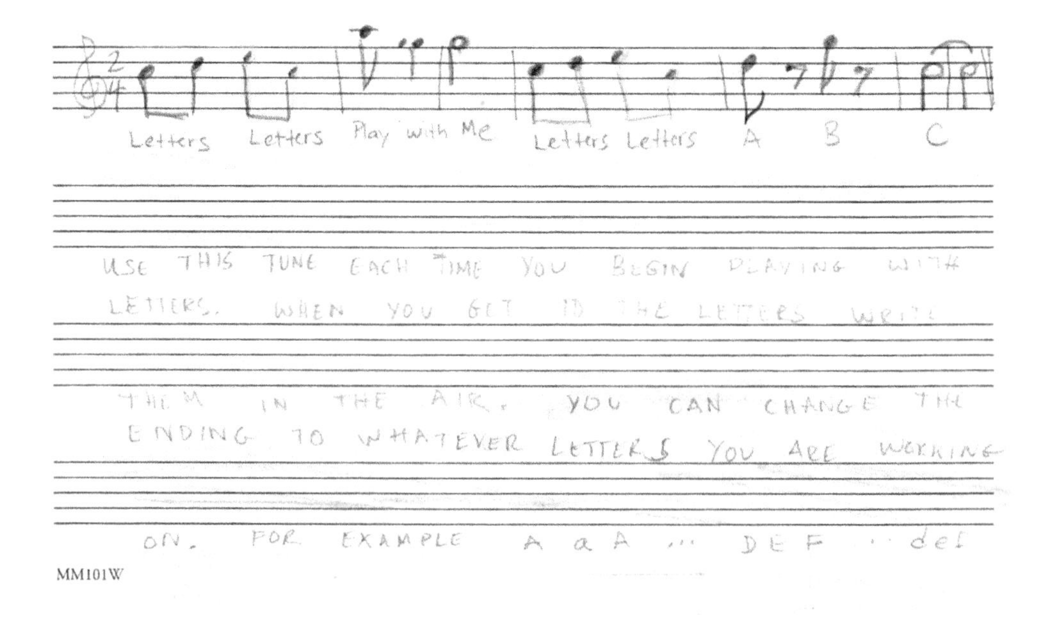

3. Next, introduce the letter as a character. Read the description. Look at the face of the letter.
4. Talk about the letter's personality. Play with the letter. (Large paper cutouts work well as do foam letters.)
5. Following personality play, ask your little one, "Hey, what does that letter say?" Review the sound(s) that the letter makes.
6. Build the letters with playdough over large letter templates. (Cut out the letter before your time together.) Foam letters also work well. Don't leave this step out. Hands-on, multisensory teaching techniques always win for all types of learners. Guide your little ones, but let them take their time. Watch how absorbed they are in the activity, and celebrate the shared focus.
7. Do a phonemic awareness exercise daily (more on this later). For now, start with reading some nursery rhymes together.
8. Close your time with the "Letters, letters, play with me" song, adding to it each time a new letter is introduced to your child. Sing the refrain after every three letters: "Letters, letters, play with me; letters, letters, A, B, C. Letters, letters, play with me; letters, letters, D, E, F," etc.

Your Starting Point

Begin the program by finding out which letters and letter sounds your child knows. You will want to end the program by doing this again. This will allow you to check your child's progress. **The number one predictor of reading readiness and future reading success is that a child can recognize letters and say their sounds sometime during kindergarten.** This is also known as breaking the phonemic code.

Here are some tips.

- First do letter identification of lower and upper case letters. Choose letters in a random pattern and mark on a sheet which ones your little one can identify.
- Next do the same for letter sounds. For vowels and two sound letters, add marks for each sound that they know.
- Relax as you ask your child to do this and you will likely notice that your child will relax too.
- Do not rush your child.
- Speak as little as possible.
- Know that this is not a measure of intelligence in any way. Symbol recognition and sound symbol correspondence happen in the brain, and for some children, the neural pathways need more repetition to develop than for others. How easily one learns to read is independent from intelligence. (You will hear more about this later.)

Now, dear reader, let's begin.

Materials Needed

You will need to get some modeling clay and/or buy or make playdough for this program. Some friends who have done the program have a preference for one or the other. Try both, and see which your child enjoys more. An interesting sidenote is that the first writers and creators of writing/reading systems wrote on clay (Sumerian cuneiform).

Here is a favorite playdough recipe. Add scents to it using essential oils. Have fun with it. As you move through the course, ask your child what the letters would smell like and what color playdough would best suit each letter, and enjoy the answers. Make more playdough!

Playdough Recipe

1 cup water
1 tablespoon vegetable oil
½ cup salt
1 tablespoon cream of tartar
Sargent Watercolor Magic™ or food coloring
1 cup flour

1. Combine water, oil, salt, cream of tartar, Sargent Watercolor Magic™ or food coloring and flour in a saucepan and heat (medium heat setting). Mix until it becomes dough.
2. Add essential oils for scents after the mixture has been removed from the stove. (Color can be added before or after removing from the stove.)
3. Your child will enjoy kneading the dough until it becomes smooth.
4. Store the dough in an airtight container or a freezer bag.

Source: https://www.familyeducational.com/fun/playdough/play-doh-recipes.

The cream of tartar makes this dough last six months or longer, so it is an important ingredient.

Letters Are Characters!©

PARENT/GUARDIAN, LET'S GET STARTED

THE IMPORTANCE OF reading cannot be overstated. This uniquely human activity is both generative and transformative. It is an occasion with the self and a way to shape our minds. Passing along a love of reading and helping our children become proficient readers is one of the most profound gifts that a caregiver can give. Reading, when done well, empowers, connects, frees, and protects. Further, shared stories strengthen our bond with our children and give us a framework to discuss tough issues. The ability to read fluently and well impacts every subject studied.

During this program, you will be on a wonderful adventure with your child. You will take the first steps of your child's journey into books hand in hand and heart to heart. How reading in the brain happens will be demystified along the way.

The first step in reading acquisition is sometimes called *cracking the phonemic code.* When this happens, children learn that words are made up of sounds (phonemes) represented by letter symbols (graphemes). For instance, the A symbol says ā (its name) and ă as in *at.* Symbol recognition (learning the letter names) and the process of attaching the sounds to the symbol takes time for children, but this ability is the best predictor of future reading success because it is an indication that the brain is ready or primed to read. They begin to grasp the underlying structure of words. This is the ultimate goal of the *Letters Are Characters* program: cracking the phonemic code and developing phonemic awareness. The other goal of this book is to make you an effective, connected first teacher and a reading advocate. Reading is the most important and essential subject that children will ever learn, and you are their most important teacher and advocate.

During your time with your child:
1. Begin with some unifying moments. Each letter has a personality, so it becomes something that you and your child can play with. (Feel free to change the personalities if they don't resonate with you and your child.) Sing the *Letters Are Characters* song as detailed previously and skywrite the letter that you are working on with your index finger.

2. After you introduce the symbol and its corresponding sound, make a letter with playdough over a letter template (ten inches for capitals and six inches for lowercase). There is a reason for the large size (more on this later).

3. When your little learner has completed the letter, do a phonemic awareness exercise. This will be explained fully later too, but for now start with something like rhyming words with your child, explaining that in rhyming the first sound is changed. Share some nursery rhymes, and see if you can say the first word and have your child say the second and so on, until you have completed the rhyme. Or try doing it with a favorite song like "Twinkle, Twinkle Little Star." (Note: Some children need explicit instruction to rhyme.)

4. Close your time with "Letters, letters, play with me; letters, letters, A, B, C..." (drawing the letters in the air as you sing them). This can be set to any tune that you can sing or you can use the melody provided. Be sure to say the A, B, C portion slowly enough to allow the children to skywrite the letters.

Reading Tip: **Reading happens in the brain and is neurological in origin. Its acquisition is independent of intelligence. Struggling readers can have high, average, or low IQs.** How fast one cracks the phonemic code depends on neural pathways. This means some children require more repetition than others. Never rush your child. If they need a full week or more to learn a letter symbol and its sound, that's fine. Don't move on to a new letter until each letter introduced is mastered. Think of it like climbing a ladder. You may find that a child's ability to get the letter and letter sound is slow at first but gets faster as you progress through the course. This indicates that the pathways are being built.

Tips for teaching your little one:
1. Make this time fun. This is a play-based concept. Kids learn best when they are relaxed and playing. Laugh, listen, and connect. Give your child your full attention.

It should be fun for you too. Leave your expectations, distractions (phone), and timetables at the door and drift along softly with your child on the current of their learning.

2. Focus on the positive. Avoid using the word "no" because it may stop or stall a child's thinking process. Instead say, "Try again," with a smile on your face. Talk about mistakes being an opportunity to learn.

3. If your child is not having fun, stop. There is an invisible string between a teacher and a student (mutual focused attention). Pay attention and observe closely if it is fraying or breaking. If it is, mix it up. Read your child a story. Take a break.

4. Be patient. It bears repeating to say that some learners could take a week or more to learn one letter. This is okay. Again, it is independent of intelligence. You are forming neural pathways that enable reading acquisition. How amazing it is that the plasticity of our brains makes us capable of incredible things like reading.

5. Read aloud to your children, preferably daily. This is one of the best ways to ensure they succeed in school. Ask them to find the letters that they have learned on the pages of the books you read together. Ask them to describe what the letters say. "Hey, what did that A just say?" Take the time to explain the meaning of unfamiliar words.

Now, plan your time to get started. It should be a time when your child is rested, fed, and able to focus. Prepare your child, saying that you are going to have "special time together." You will need your large letter foam or template (at least ten inches for uppercase and six inches for lowercase) and your playdough. Let's get started.

Note on the illustrations: The illustrations are simple and hand drawn for a reason. Your child should be able to draw and color them, as well as play with their facial expressions and change their look if they so desire. For example, one little friend decided that P should wear purple and pink because those colors begin with P.

A is a vowel. He is a two-sound guy.

Pronounce the short vowel (ă sound) when you see a lowercase letter and the long vowel (ā sound) when you see a capital letter.

Daddy A likes to be first.
When he can't be, his mood is the worst!
He says (ă and ā). "When I am not first, I am a-a-aggravated! I need to be the leader! When the word starts with a-a-a like *at*, it is great. But not when it is b-a-t or c-a-t, bat the *b* and cut that *c*. Let me a-a-at 'em. I am the leader, the number one letter in the a-a-alphabet, and when I am a-a-angry, I act like a mad Ape."

And when the letters don't move out of the w-a-y, A uses his long sound to boss people around. (Insert the long sound of A here). A, A, A, A, A, get out of the wAy. Move W, A!

His little son, baby a, looks on and says, "A, a, a. D-a-d, Dad, I am going to grow up to be just like you!'"

Personality trait: Aggravated
Favorite food: Apple

Parent Tips: Pronounce short vowel sounds when you see the lowercase letter and long vowel sounds when you see the capital letter. Explain that every word needs a vowel and that this is the first vowel they will meet.

Also, do not move to *b* until *a* is mastered. Your learner first should be able to make the letter in clay over the letter form, then do it while looking at the letter, and lastly produce the letter without the letter form present. Your learner should be able to say the sounds and describe the personality before moving on. Play games with bossy A. At this stage of development, children love a chance to play with a naughty character because it holds a certain fascination. It is funny to children who are learning the rules to see them broken. When teaching lowercase *a*, you can show your learner that *a* can look different in typed fonts versus handwriting. (Baby a sometimes looks like this: ***a*** in print and **a** when you write it.)

Aa

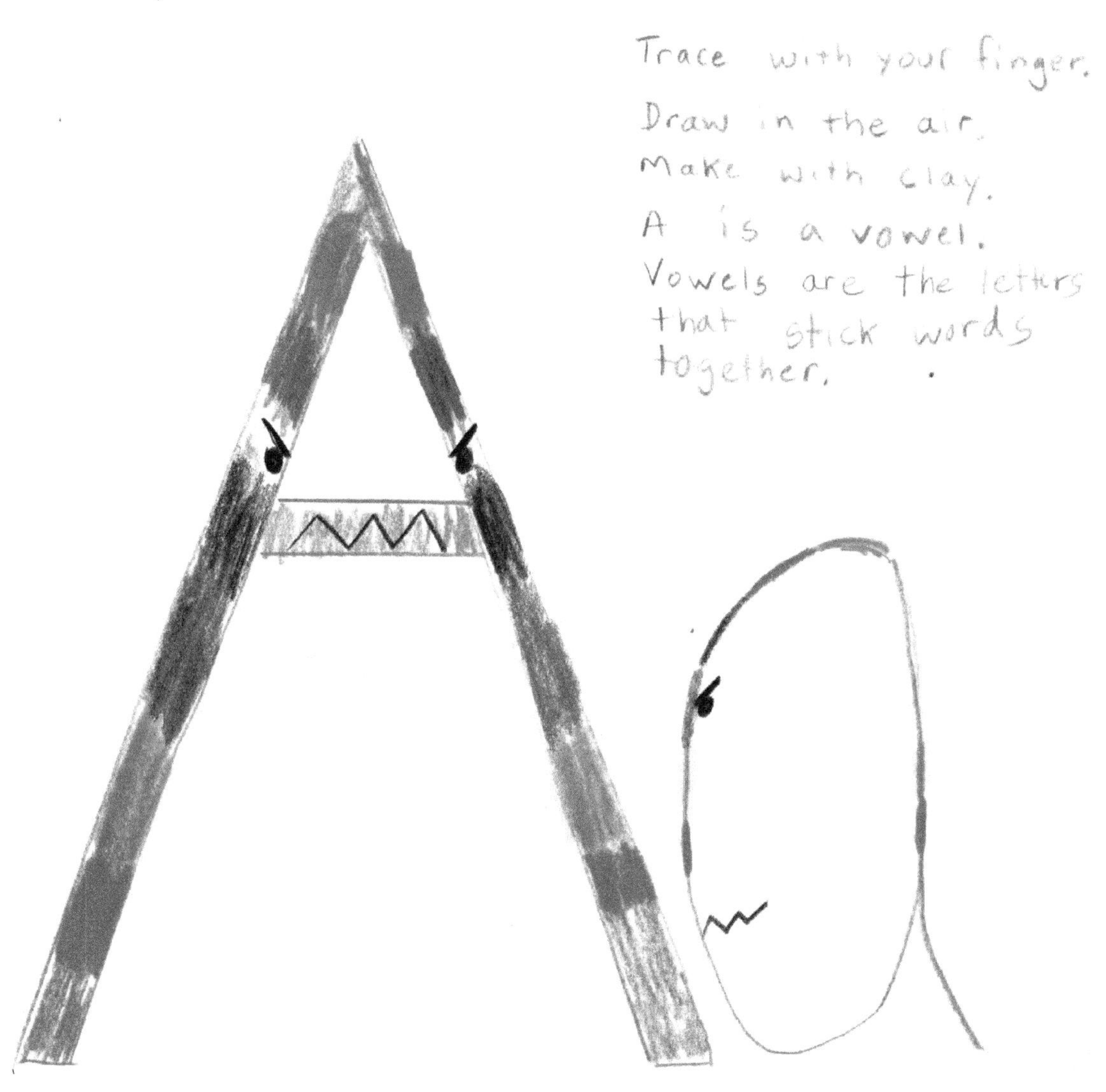

All vowels are multicolored because they do lots of jobs and make more than one sound.

B is a consonant. She is a one-sound gal.

Mommy B loves to bounce down and up! But she doesn't always watch where she is going.

She says (insert *b* sound here). "I like to go b-b-boing when I b-b-bounce.
Sometimes when I bop in and go b-b-boom, the other letters say things like, 'Hey, B, watch where you are going! The word was *at*, and you bounced in and made it b-a-t! Come back later when it is time for a b-b-ball game.'"
So B says, "Bye, I'll be b-b-back," and off she bounces.

Cute little baby b looks on, sucking on her binky, and says, "Mama, I am going to grow up and be bouncy and go boing just like you!"

Personality trait: Bouncy
Favorite food: Broccoli

Parent Tips: Your emerging reader should be able to first make the letter in clay over the letter form, then beside it, and then without it. Try writing the letter. Your reader should be able to say the sounds and describe the personality of *b* before you move on. Make *b* bounce into things dramatically and make a mess. Review *a*, and play with what would happen when *a* meets *b*.

Baby B can hide in his mom's belly!

This trick may help little readers remember.

b and d are tricky to tell apart.

C is a consonant. He is a two-sound guy.

He sounds like K when he sits beside a, o, or u, and he sounds like S when he sits beside e, i, or y.

Daddy C is very cute. He likes to curve around his friends and give cuddles.

He says (insert hard *k* sound) and (insert soft *s* sound). "I love to c-c-cuddle and c-c-care and give c-c-comfort. I love everyone to be c-c-calm and c-c-cooperate. Sitting next to *i*, *e*, or *y* makes me sound like an *s*, so I c-c-celebrate!" Having two sounds is fun for c-c-caring c-c-citizen C!

Little baby boy c is c-c-curious as a baby c should be. He says, "Dad, c-c-come and c-c-connect with me." Daddy comes and hugs his boy (Cc), and they fit so comfortably.

Personality trait: Caring
Favorite food: Celery and carrots

Parent Tips: Wait to move on to *d* until *a*, *b*, and c are mastered. Build in time to review. Play games with *a*, *b*, and *c*, exploring what happens when they meet. This shows kids how phonemes work. A phoneme is the smallest unit of sound: C. A. B. *Cab* is made up of three sounds or phonemes. This must be taught explicitly because if you were to see the sound wave form of the word, you would not see the boundaries between the letters. You are teaching your child to map sounds, which is an abstraction.

Your learner should be able to make the letters over the forms, beside the letter forms, and independently. Try writing the letters. Take your time!

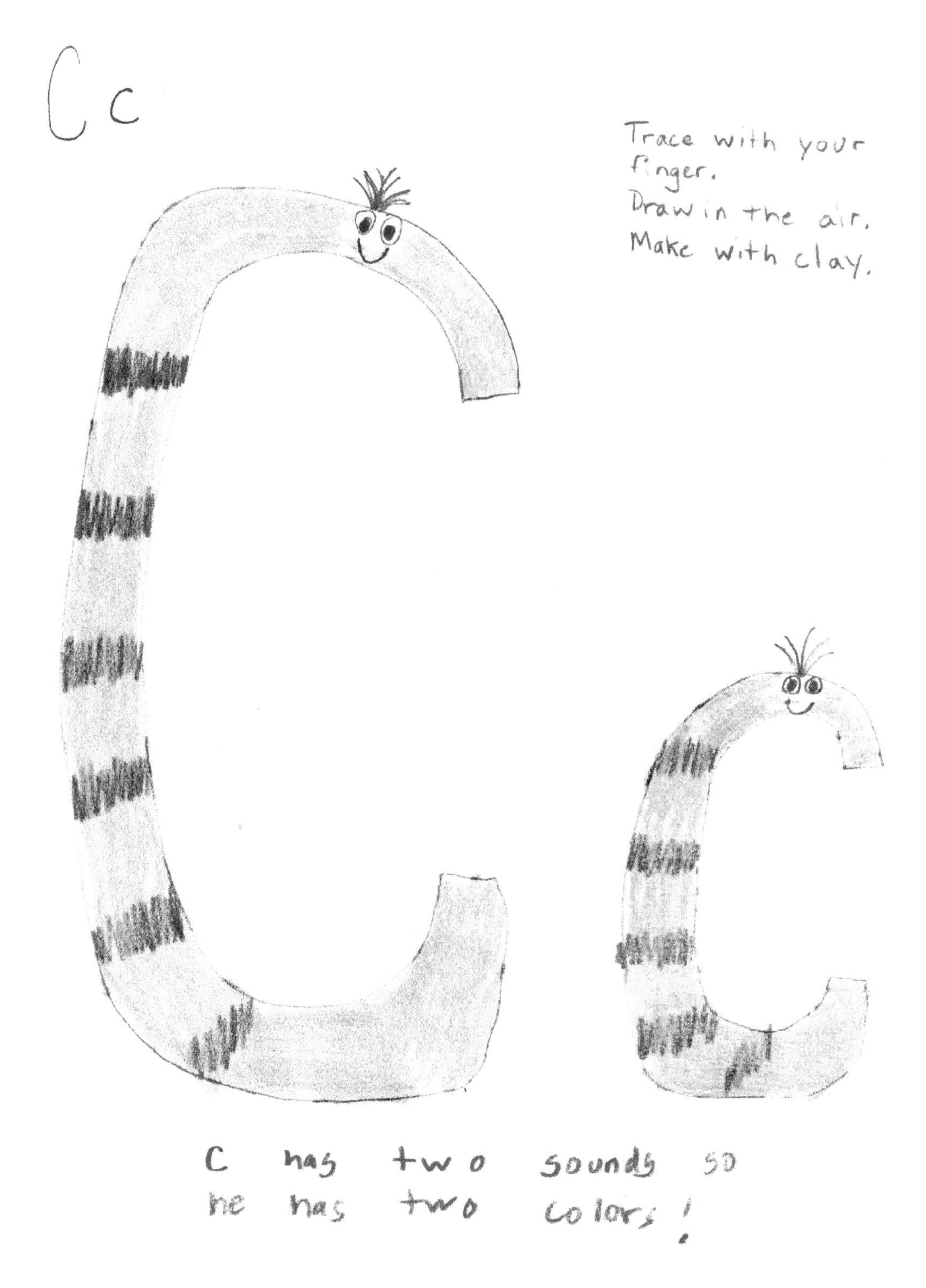
Cc
Trace with your finger.
Draw in the air.
Make with clay.
C has two sounds so he has two colors!

Letters Are Characters!©

Parent/Guardian—Phonemic Awareness

So, what is a phoneme anyway? A phoneme is the smallest unit of speech that corresponds to a letter or group of letters. Phonemes are abstractions from spoken words that enable us to read and write them. For instance, the word *cat* is made up of three phonemes: c–a-t. Adding complexity for children is the fact that some combinations of letters make only one phoneme. For example, in the word *chip*, there are four letters but only three phonemes: ch-i-p. In English there are twenty-six letters and more than forty-four phonemes (not all researchers agree on that number). If our alphabet had forty-four characters, we could have one for each phoneme, but since we have twenty-six characters, some letters and letter combinations make more than one phoneme.

In order to be able to process the pairing of sounds to letter symbols (B says *b*—put your hand in front of your mouth to feel the exhalation, versus D says *d*—no breath), children must understand that spoken language is made up of these little sounds that are in words. Explicit instruction to develop phonemic awareness is always better than assuming that little ones will implicitly grasp this concept. Children learn speech by imitation, but reading must be taught. Research indicates that not all children can recognize that words can be broken apart into little sounds and that strings of sounds make language. Approximately 25 percent of children will struggle quite a bit in this area. Many children may grasp the meaning of the word but be stymied if asked to break it into its component sounds. This causes difficulty for reading acquisition, writing, comprehension, and spelling. It is important to understand that all children will benefit from phonemic awareness games and exercises, and for some, they are essential.

How can we get children to notice phonemes? Rhyming and playing games involving sounds, which children love and naturally gravitate to, is an effective way to get them to play and develop phonemic awareness. There is much research that confirms that children who are provided this kind of explicit listening instruction in pre-K and kindergarten are much more successful readers/spellers in first grade. Teach them to listen for sameness, difference, number, and order of sounds. Talk about accents, inflection, and pronunciation.

Many researchers have found that lack of phonemic awareness in grade one predicted poor readers in grade four. This is a skill that can be taught but requires specific methods and lots of repetition. Home is the ideal place for parent-child phonemic awareness-building games.

When teaching phonemes, use your thumb and fingers on one hand to tap them. Teach your little one to do the same. Later clap syllables so your learner can distinguish more easily between phonemes and syllables.

Additionally, it is important to build phonological awareness. This means explaining that sentences are made up of words; words are made up of syllables; and phonemes, or the smallest units of sound, make up words.

Phonemic awareness goes hand in hand with learning to read and spell. During each session or special time with your child, include some phonemic awareness exercises and games.

Resources to use at home:

Adams, Marilyn Jager, Barbara R. Foorman, Ingvar Lundberg, and Terri Beller. 2014. *Phonemic Awareness in Young Children.* Baltimore: Paul H. Brookes Publishing Co.

Earobics Step 1, Home Version: Sound Foundations for Reading & Spelling. 1997. Houghton Mifflin (available on Amazon).

D is a consonant. She is a one-sound gal.

Mommy D is daring. She brags about her deeds.

She says (insert *d* sound here). "Why, I am delighted with myself!
I am d-d-divine and d-d-dreamy. I am d-d-dandy and so d-d-dazzling!"
D has a weakness. She can't turn down a dare. So when the other letters feel mischievous, D needs to beware.

Baby d is d-d-dedicated to her d-d-dandy mom, and she says, "When I grow up, I will be divine just like you!"

Personality trait: Dazzling and dandy
Favorite food: Doughnuts

Parent tips: Do not move on to *e* until *a*, *b*, *c*, and *d* are mastered. Play games with *a*, *b*, *c*, and *d*, exploring what happens when they meet. Have D and A argue about who should go first. Have them shout their sounds. Review the personalities of each letter. Ask your learner to make a cape for D. A child might use a tissue or a washcloth or come up with something new. Spend some time working with lowercase *b* and *d*. Explain that *c* likes to try to cuddle *d* to calm her down. Put *c* over lowercase *d* to demonstrate. Review baby b fitting in his mom's tummy. This may help them remember how to write the characters.

Your learner should be able to make the letters over the forms, beside the letter forms, and independently. Try writing the letters. Take your time!

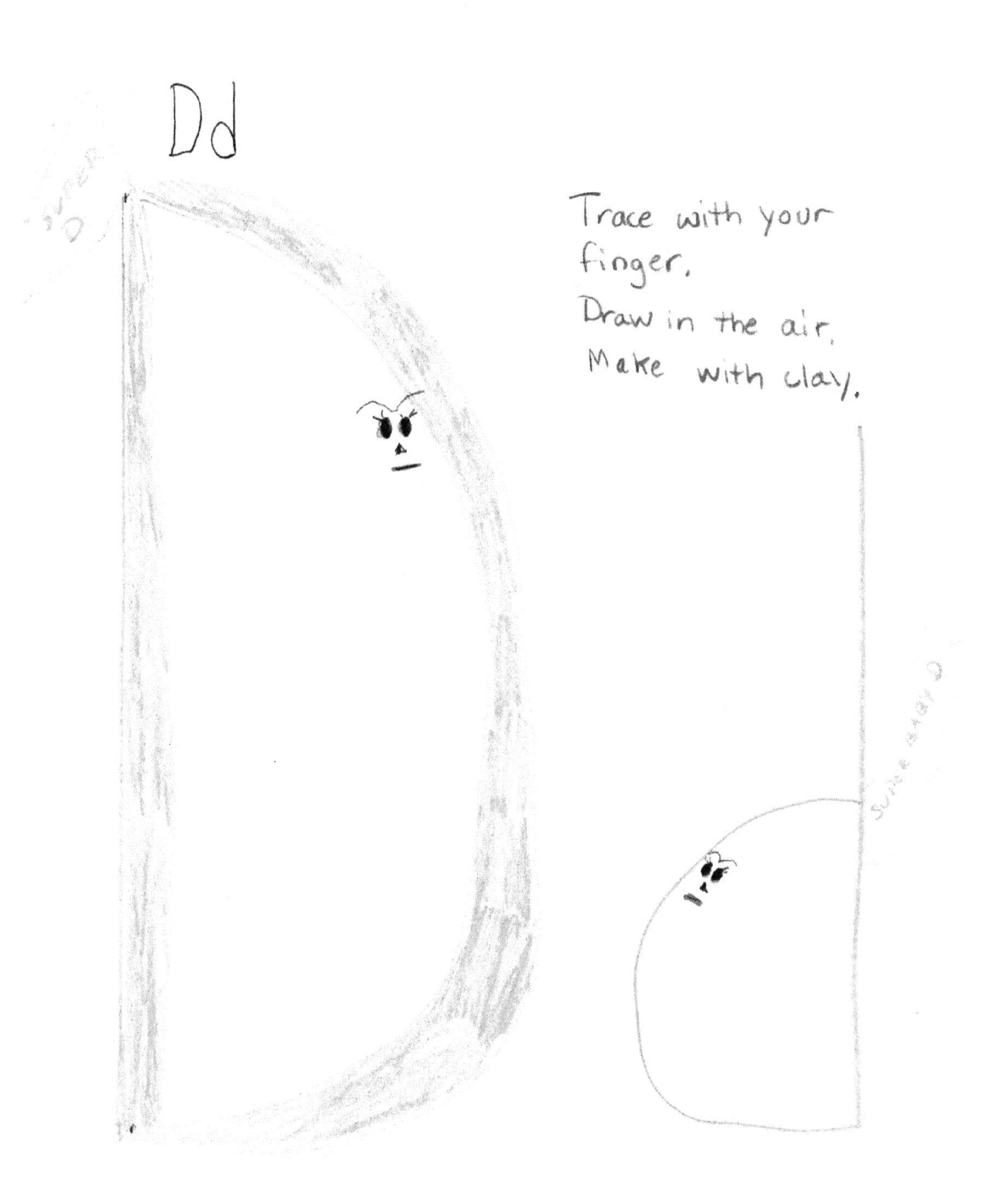

Baby c and baby d are pals. c can jump onto d and they fly together! c → d. This trick can help little readers remember how to make d.

E is a vowel. He is a two-sound guy.

Daddy E is scared every day. But he can be the bravest for all of his friends, quietly empowering them.

He says (insert short vowel sound ĕ as in *elephant* and ē, which is his name). He says, "Eeeeeee," as if he has seen a ghost and "e-e-e" to empower himself. "I am frightened e-e-endlessly; it is true. But when I think of my friends, I am E-E-Eager to get in and help, and I stop thinking of myself."

Little baby e looks on and beams at his dad. He is e-e-encouraging and E-E-Eager to please, just like his dad.

Personality trait: Eager and empathetic
Favorite food: Eggplant

Parent tip: Pronounce the short vowel sound when you see a lowercase letter and the long vowel sound when you see a capital letter.

Parent tip: Do not move on to *f* until *a*, *b*, *c*, *d*, and *e* are are mastered. Play games with *a*, *b*, *c*, and *d*, exploring what happens when they meet *e*. Put *e* between *b* and *d*. Show the *b* and *d* with your left and right hand. This may help your learner remember the direction. Put *e* at end of a word like *mad* and explain that if *e* is at the end of the word (*made*), he makes the middle vowel feel brave enough to shout out his long sound, and then he sits down at the end of the word and doesn't make a peep. Review the personalities of each letter. Let your learner shout, "Eeeee!" and have fun with that scared long sound.

Your learner should be able to make the letters over the forms, beside the letter forms, and independently. Try writing the letters. Take your time!

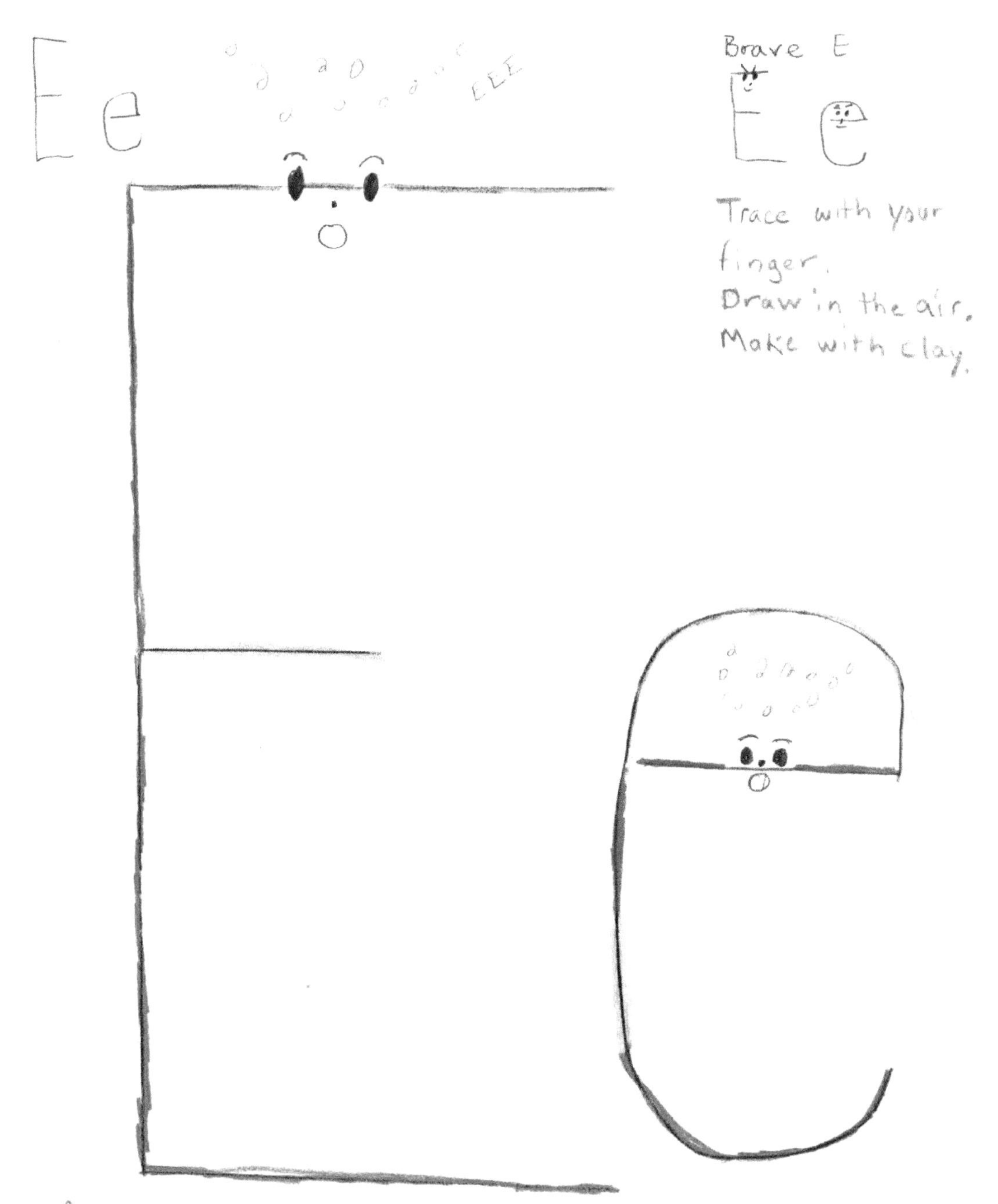

All vowels are multicolored because the do lots of jobs and make more than one sound. E can be brave too! When he sits at the end of words he helps vowels say their long sounds!

Letters Are Characters!©

On Reading

"Children are made readers on the laps of their parents."
—Emilie Buchwald

Reading Tip #1: Help spread the word. Many people think that smart kids learn to read easily, and this is not true. Smart kids may or may not learn to read easily. Struggling readers can have low, average, or genius IQs. Reading happens in the brain and is neurological in origin. Its acquisition is independent of intelligence. How fast one begins to read depends on neural pathways – how the brain processes the smallest units of sound that make up words. This means some children require more repetition of evidence-based methods than others.

Reading Tip #2: All children learn best from explicit instruction on letter sounds and language structure when learning to read (phonics and morphology—more on this later). Phonics-based instruction is important for all learners and essential for more than 20 percent.

Reading Tip #3: The best time for early reading intervention is age five and six. (Rapid automatized naming and other tests can be used to determine potential struggling readers before they even begin to learn to read). If your child is having difficulty recognizing symbols and attaching the letter sounds to the symbols, don't wait to begin intervention. If there are struggling readers or dyslexics in your family, pay attention (dyslexia is genetic). It will be within your grasp and capabilities to be part of the team as you progress through this course. Don't let any institution tell you to leave it to them. Your child spends the most time with you.

Reading Tip #4: A parent/caregiver knows his or her child best. Your involvement can make all of the difference for a child who is struggling to read. Parents/caregivers must be part of the process as they are the constant in a child's life.

Researchers estimate that more than 40 percent of American children are not reaching fluency benchmarks by fourth grade. Parents and community involvement can change this in the future.

Best practices in reading instruction for all children are the following:

- Explicit—reading is explained step by step.
- Repetitive—instruction is repeated until each new concept is mastered. Daily reading instruction helps to build neural pathways that enable reading in the brain. (Thirty-plus minutes are best, including phonemic awareness, phonics, writing characters, etc.)
- Multisensory—instruction involves as many senses as possible (olfactory, tactile, auditory, visual, and even taste). The brain stores and retrieves memories in a variety of ways, including each of the senses (Wolf, 2008).
- One-on-one or small group—a parent or caregiver can make all of the difference. Carve out some time each day to work on reading acquisition. Keep notes on your child's progress so you can focus on what they need.

In addition to working on reading acquisition with your little learner, one of the very best things you can do at home is read to your child.

If we read to our children, they are likely to

- do better in school;
- be more empathetic;
- be happier;
- develop a stronger bond with you;
- develop imagination and creativity;
- have improved language skills;
- be better at thinking, understanding, reasoning, and problem-solving;
- have a framework to talk about tough issues; and
- be more likely to read for fun.

Creating the Reading Habit

What your child needs most for healthy development is a strong, solid bond with their caregivers. The greatest gift that you can give them is your time and attention. Much of what we do as humans is generated from routines and habits. Read with your children every day to build the framework that will serve them well for a lifetime.

- Choose a special, cozy reading space.
- Read every day at about same time so it will form a healthy habit and routine. Bedtime stories are a great way to end the day.
- Choose books together, talk about interests, and talk about the book.
- Explain the meaning of unfamiliar words.
- Use the illustrations as a way to talk about the story.
- **Read to your children even when they are babies**. Very young babies love to hear the sound of a familiar voice and absorb much that helps their developing brains.
- Don't stop reading to your children once they can read on their own. Older children still need to be read to in order to develop rich vocabularies and have a context provided so they can discuss their thoughts. Despite popular practice, children still need reading instruction to achieve optimal fluency after third grade.
- Ask your child questions to check their comprehension during the reading. "What do you think the character is feeling now?" "What do you think will happen next?"
- Make your time fun. Kids learn best when they are relaxed and playing. Laugh together.
- If your child loses interest, refocus by gently asking your child to find something on the page or choose another book.

There is much scientific research on how we learn to read. These are three great books:

Dehaene, Stanislas. 2009. *Reading in the Brain.* New York: Viking.
Seidenberg, Mark. 2017. *Language at the Speed of Sight.* New York: Basic Books.
Wolf, Maryanne. 2008. *The Story and Science of the Reading Brain.* New York: Harper.

A good, free learning app is StarFall.
http://www.starfall.com/

A great one you can buy is "Learning with Homer."
https://learnwithhomer.com

Use this Page for Notes, Doodles and Drawings

F is a consonant. She is a one-sound gal.
Mommy F is fearless. She makes E feel safe, and she looks like E without his bottom line. She can fly.

She says (insert *f* sound here). "Have no f-f-fear, E! F-f-for I am here! You are my f-f-favorite, and you are a true f-f-friend. Let's f-f-fly and make everyone f-f-feel f-f-free!"

Little baby f puts on her f-f-fantastic F costume with a cape and says, "F-f-flawless, f-f-fearless Mom, I will be f-f-fit and f-f-fabulous just like you."

Personality trait: Fabulous
Favorite food: French fries

Parent tip: Do not move on to *g* until *a*, *b*, *c*, *d*, *e*, and *f* are mastered. Play games with *a*, *b*, *c*, *d*, *e*, and *f*. Have *f* fly and take *e* with her. Put f-a-b together and review the sounds. Explain that F is *fab*ulous. Review the personalities of each letter.

Your learner should be able to make the letters over the forms, beside the letter forms, and independently. Try writing the letters. Take your time!

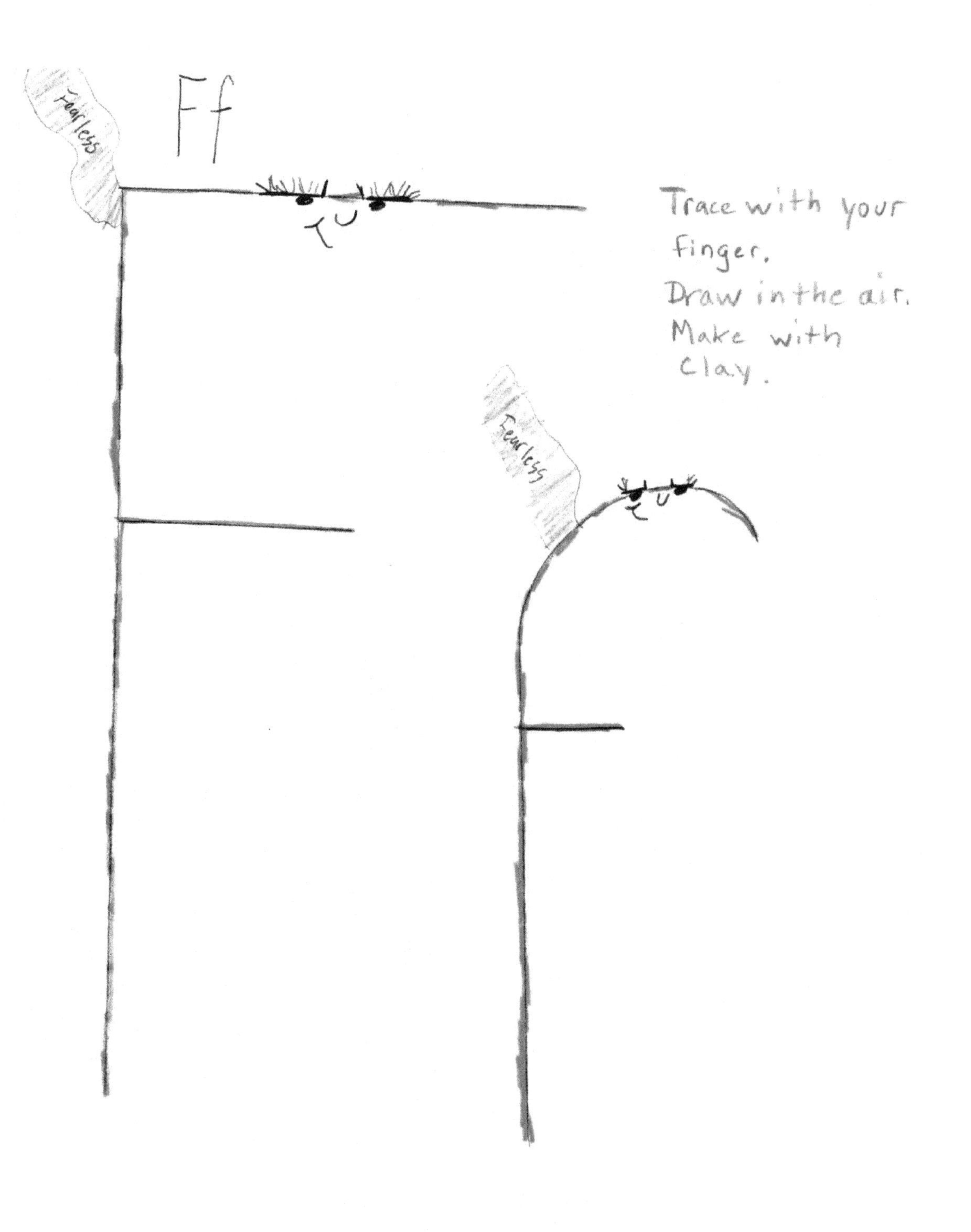
Ff
Fearless
Trace with your finger.
Draw in the air.
Make with clay.
Fearless

G is a consonant. He is a two-sound guy.

G is great and loves to give.

He says (insert hard sound of G as in *game*) and sometimes (insert soft sound of *j* as in *gem*). "I love to g-g-give g-g-gifts to all of my g-g-great friends. It makes me g-g-giggle! It is the way that I show my friends how g-g-grateful I am for them. They are g-g-gems. One little thing that I like to g-g-give my friends is their hair g-g-gel!"

Little baby g listens to his dad and says, "Daddy, your g-g-great heart is g g-giant. When I grow up, I am g-g-going to be g-g-generous just like you!"

Personality trait: Generous
Favorite food: Grapes

Parent tip: Do not move on to *h* until *a*, *b*, *c*, d, *e*, *f*, and *g* are mastered. Play games with *a*, *b*, *c*, *d*, *e*, *f*, and *g*. Compare C and G because the rule is the same: G generally uses his soft sound when sitting next to *e*, *i*, or *y* and his hard sound when sitting beside *a*, *o*, or *u*. Ask your learner to make both sounds—*g* as in *gem* and *g* as in *gut*. Ask them to put their hand on their throat to feel the difference. Practice having G play a game with another letter and giving him a gem for a prize.

Your learner should be able to make the letters over the forms, beside the letter forms, and independently. Try writing the letters. Take your time!

Gg
G uses hair gel
giggle giggle
Trace with your finger.
Draw in the air.
Make with clay.
G has two sounds so he has two colors!

H is a consonant. She is a one-sound gal.

Mommy H is the happiest letter around. She loves to be helpful and say hello.

"I think being h-h-happy is h-h-healthy. I spread joy wherever I go, and it usually starts with a smile and a simple h-h-hi or h-h-hello. The letters that are crabby, I try to make h-h-harmonious!"

Little baby h waits to grow her top line. She looks at her mom with a giant smile and says in a baby voice, "H-h-hi, h-h-happy Mommy! I am going to grow up and be h-h-harmonious just like you!"

Personality trait: Happy
Favorite food: Hamburgers

Parent tip: Do not move on to *i* until *a*, *b*, *c*, *d*, *e*, *f*, *g*, and *h* are mastered. Play games with *a*, *b*, *c*, *d*, *e*, *f*, *g*, and *h* to review their sounds. See if your child can remember all of their favorite foods. Stress the first sound. Ask your child to put their hand in front of their mouth and feel their breath as the say the *h* in h-h-happy.

Your learner should be able to make the letters over the forms, beside the letter forms, and independently. Try writing the letters. Take your time!

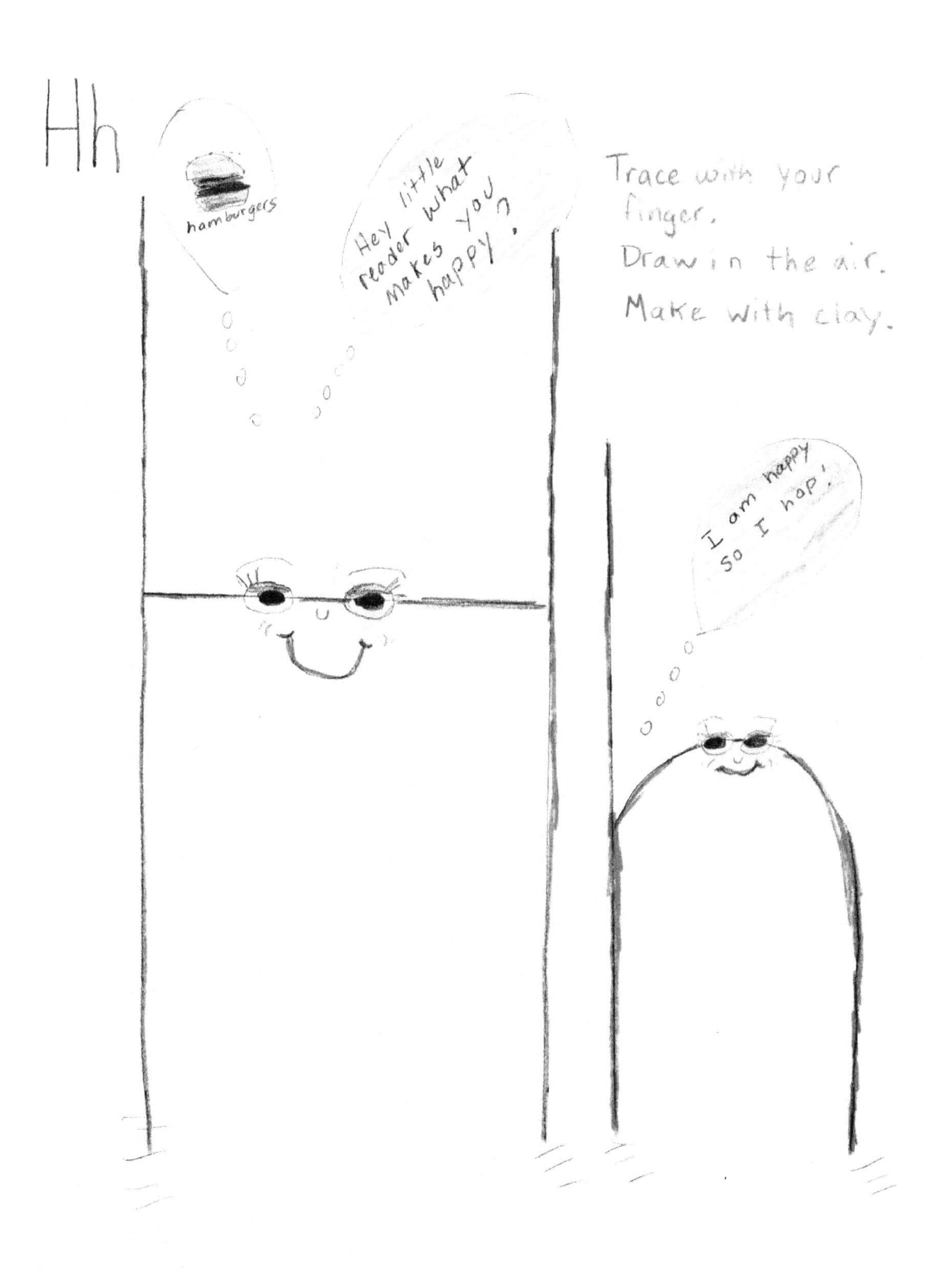
Hh
hamburgers
Hey little reader what makes you happy?
Trace with your finger.
Draw in the air.
Make with clay.
I am happy so I hop!

Letters Are Characters!©

Why Faces on the Letters? And Personalities?

Why use *characters with stories* to teach about letter *characters*? Because reading is a relatively modern adaptation of our brains. It happens in specific *repurposed* areas of the brain. Being able to recognize familiar faces, and knowing who is a friend or a foe and their stories is a well-established function of our brains. Some of the letter characters are really naughty, and there is a reason for this too. Our brains have a "negativity bias." We remember the bad guys because our brains react more strongly to negative stimuli (see the work of John Cacioppo, PhD). Also, letters are presented as large objects because one of the reading parts of the brain is a repurposed area used for object recognition. (Large letters can be fashioned from most anything, but they should be three dimensional and have a pleasing texture.)

Mothers and babies will spend countless hours gazing lovingly at each other's faces. Children delight in hearing stories. People have been sharing stories for tens of thousands of years. There is a rich body of research on the brain basis for our human connection to stories (e.g., see Paul Zak PhD). Stories trigger a specific chain of events in the brain and body. Our heart rate increases when we listen, and then the brain secretes oxytocin, the neurochemical known for its ability to promote bonding. We continue to listen. Our brains, minds, and hearts are changed by stories. They generate our thoughts and shape our "selves." Storytelling triggers self-awareness and empathy. It teaches us. To be human means that *we must make meaning*, and stories help us create it.

Additionally, stories relax children, and this creates optimal learning conditions. Reading acquisition is serious—the learning of every subject is contingent upon its acquisition. Its seriousness mandates that it be taught playfully to young children for whom play is essential. We need our children to love to read, and making it a playful process is the optimal way. Children are expected to learn nine thousand words by third grade. By fourth grade they are expected to read with fluency. Sadly, we are failing to reach this goal for the majority of our learners (see Wolf, 2008; Proust; and the Squid). We need more than just our schools to be involved in finding solutions. Parents need to be an empowered part of the process. We can make all of the difference with fun, at-home intervention that has ripple-effect benefits, including strong parent/child bonds. Without early intervention, vocabulary lags behind; therefore, comprehension does too.

Parent tip: Make up stories with the letter characters that resonate with your child. Feel free to change the character traits and personalities so they work for your learner.

Note: When we read deeply, the same areas of our brain are stimulated as when we experience a situation.

I is a vowel. He is a two-sound guy.

Daddy I is so selfish. He just thinks about what he wants all day long and ignores everything else.

He says (insert short sound of ĭ) and (insert long sound of ī). "I don't care who wants what I-I-I want! I get bored when I need to listen i-i-intently to others because i-i-it is not i-i-interesting. I am interesting, and I want to sit with my i-i-iguana in an i-i-igloo and eat i-i-ice cream now!"

His son, little baby i, blinks his dot at his dad and says, "I want more too, and I want to grow up and be i-i-interesting just like you!"

Personality trait: Interesting (to himself)
Favorite food: Ice cream

Parent tip: Do not move on to *j* until *a*, *b*, *c*, *d*, *e*, *f*, *g*, *h*, and *i* are mastered. Play games with *a*, *b*, *c*, *d*, *e*, *f*, *g*, *h*, and *i* to review their sounds. See if your child can describe their personalities. Ask your child what would happen if A and I met. Would they argue? What about if happy H met I?

Parent tip: Pronounce a short vowel sound when you see a lowercase letter and a long vowel sound when you see a capital letter.

Your learner should be able to make the letters over the forms, beside the letter forms, and independently. Try writing the letters. Take your time!

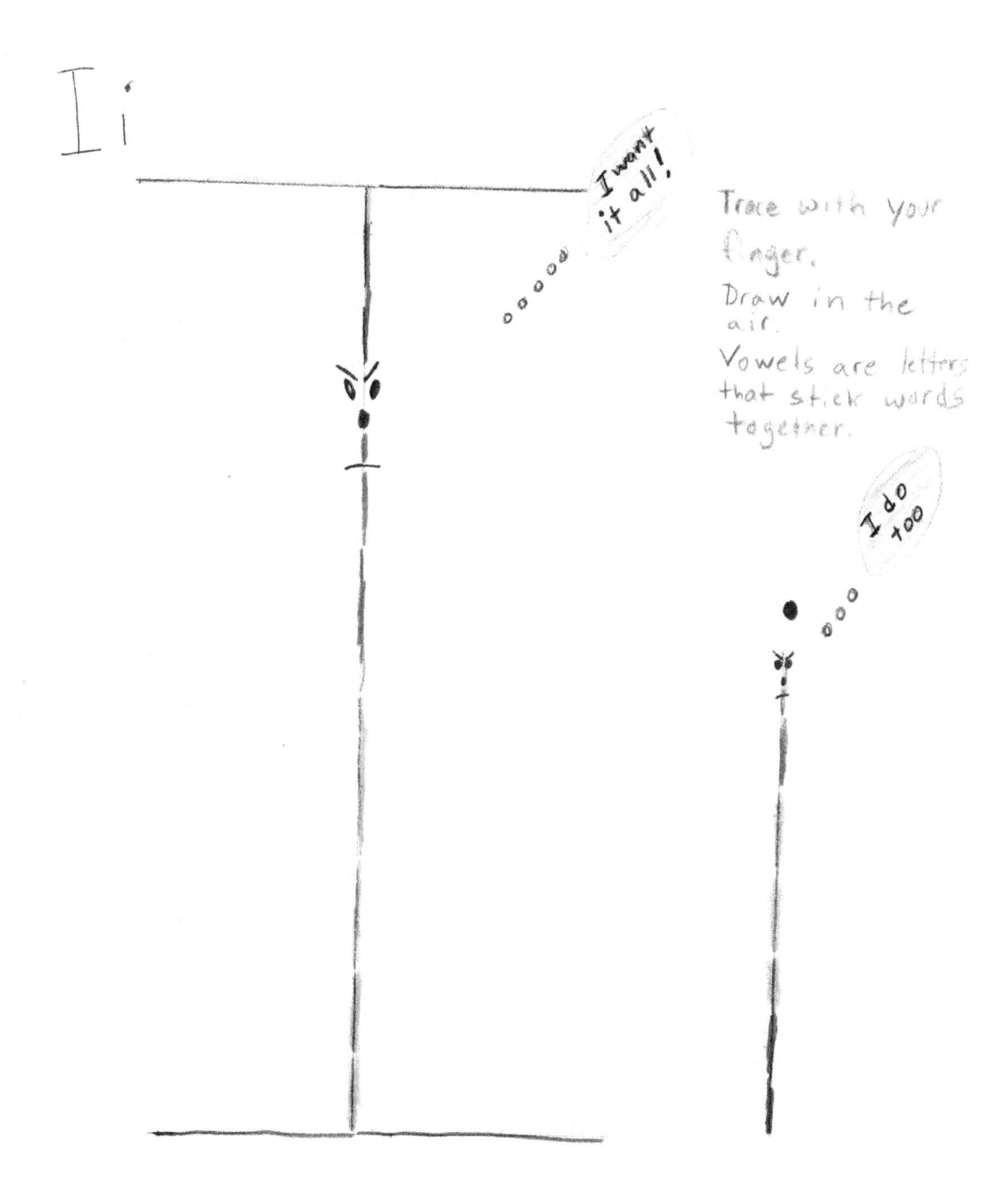

All vowels are multicolored because they do lots of jobs and make more than one sound.

J is a consonant. She is a one-sound gal.

Mommy J loves her job. She looks like the letter I but with a jolly hook. And her job is to catch letters and jumble them up. She is full of mischief, this gal, and if words on a page are all mixed up, Pirate J was at work.

She says (insert j sound here). "I love my hook; it gives me j-j-joy to catch other letters and give them a j-j-jiggle. I j-j-jostle and j-j-jab and make the words j-j-jump and j-j-jig. Arrggg! I am J, and a j-j-jumbling pirate I is!"
So J shakes her hook and dives back in a book. J, ahoy!

Baby j wiggles her little hook and does a j-j-joyful j-j-jig. "Someday I will be j-j-just like my mom!"

Personality trait: Jumpy
Favorite food: Jawbreakers

Parent tip: Do not move on to *k* until *a, b, c, d, e, f, g, h, i,* and *j* are mastered. Play games with *a, b, c, d, e, f, g, h, i,* and *j* to review their sounds. See if your child can describe their personalities. Have J and baby j jumble up a bunch of letters and make a mess. Try to juggle the *j*'s.

Your learner should be able to make the letters over the forms, beside the letter forms, and independently. Try writing the letters. Take your time!

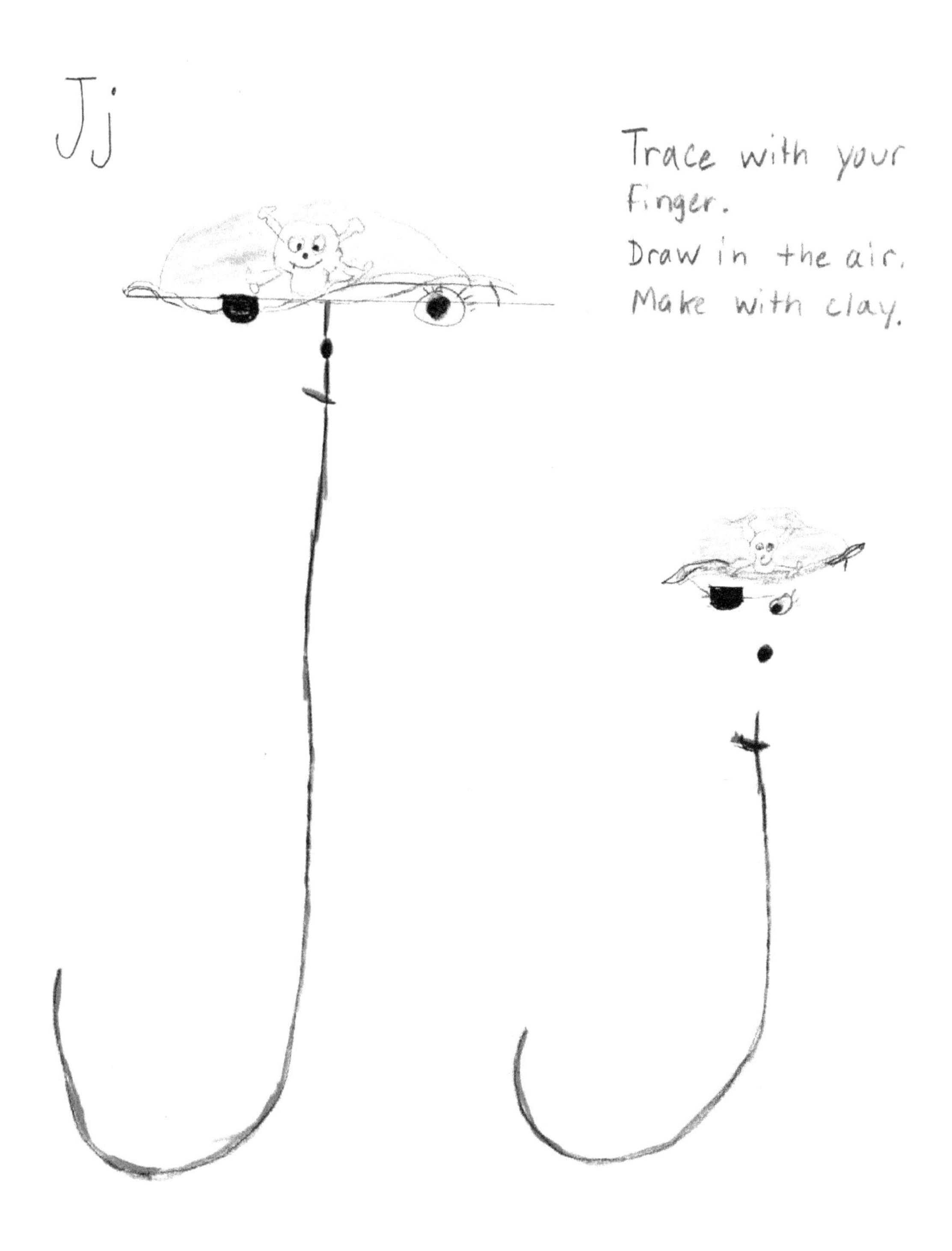
Jj
Trace with your finger.
Draw in the air.
Make with clay.

K is a consonant. He is a one-sound guy.

Daddy K may be the naughtiest letter of all because what he wants to do all day long is kick.

He says (insert *k* sound here). "I love to k-k-kick, and I've got the shape for it. No k-k-kisses for me! Be it a ball or a k-k-kid, kicking is my thing, and I will even k-k-kick down the k-k-kindergarten door. I am not known for k-k-kindness! Not me! I love k-k-karate."

Little son k looks on, practices his karate kicks, and says, "Someday, Daddy, I will kick you too! Dad, can I kick you?"

Personality trait: Kooky and kicky
Favorite food: Kebabs

Parent tip: Do not move on to *l* until *a, b, c, d, e, f, g, h, i, j,* and *k* are mastered. Play games with *a, b, c, d, e, f, g, h, i, j,* and *k* to review their sounds. Have K gently kick your learner in the foot, and let them try making K kick. Talk about what K's shoe collection might look like.

Your learner should be able to make the letters over the forms, beside the letter forms, and independently. Try writing the letters. Take your time!

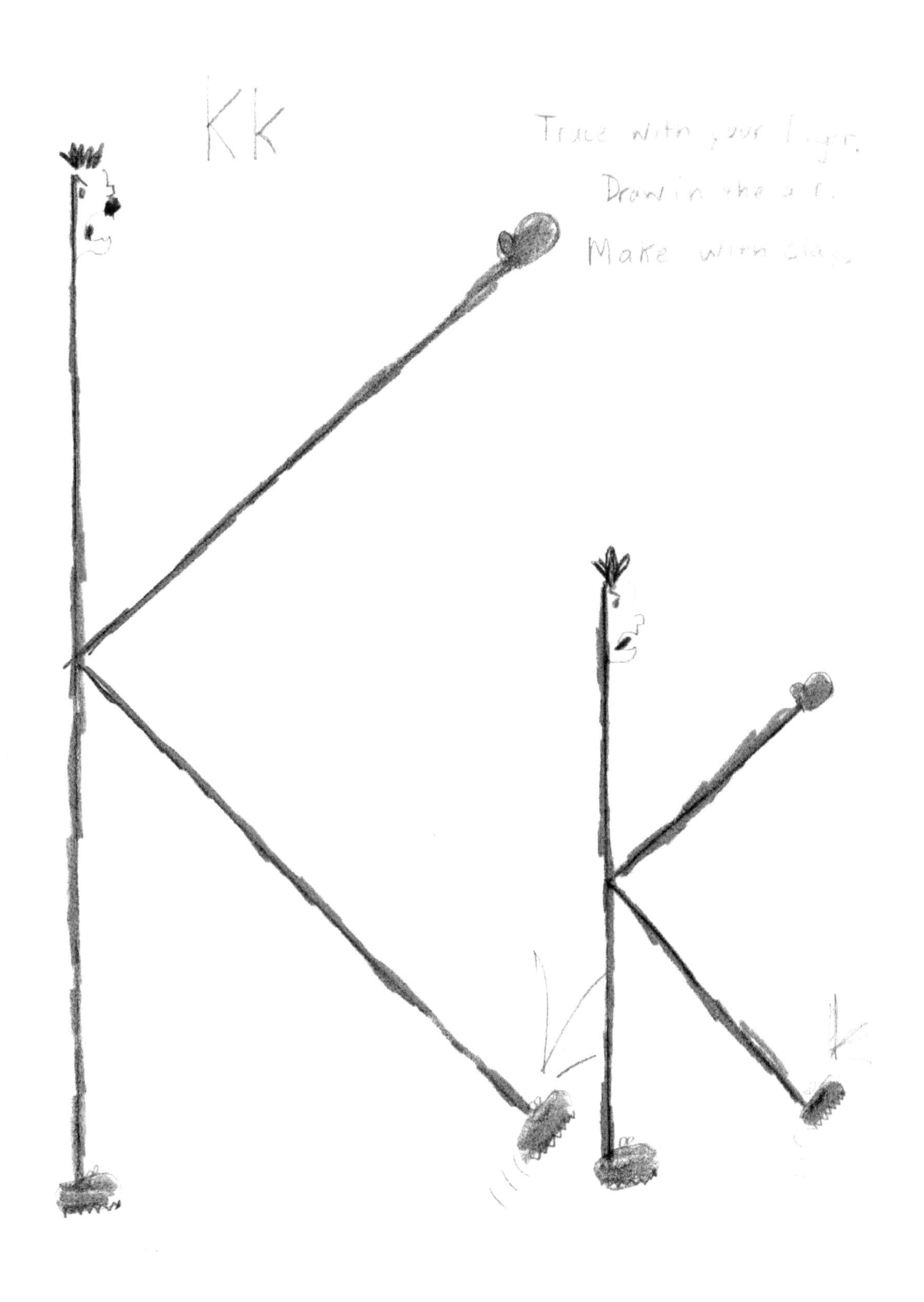
Kk
Trace with your finger.
Draw in the air.
Make with clay.
k

L is a consonant. She is a one-sound gal.

Mommy L is full of Love. She is the most loving letter of all. She likes and loves everyone.

She says (insert *l* sound here). "I know the secret of l-l-life is l-l-love. The more you give, the more you l-l-learn that l-l-love brings a special l-l-luck, for no matter what, if you l-l-love, you are l-l-lovely."

Little baby l l-l-looks at Mom, and hearts squeeze out from her tippity top. She says with a l-l-lisp, "Mommy, I l-l-love you l-l-loads. I will be just like you when I grow up."

Personality trait: Loving
Favorite food: Lollipops

Parent tip: Do not move on to *m* until *a, b, c, d, e, f, g, h, i, j, k,* and *l* are mastered. Play games with *a, b, c, d, e, f, g, h, i, j, k,* and *l* to review their sounds. Play with L and K together. Would they get along? How would L try to teach K?

Your learner should be able to make the letters over the forms, beside the letter forms, and independently. Try writing the letters. Take your time!

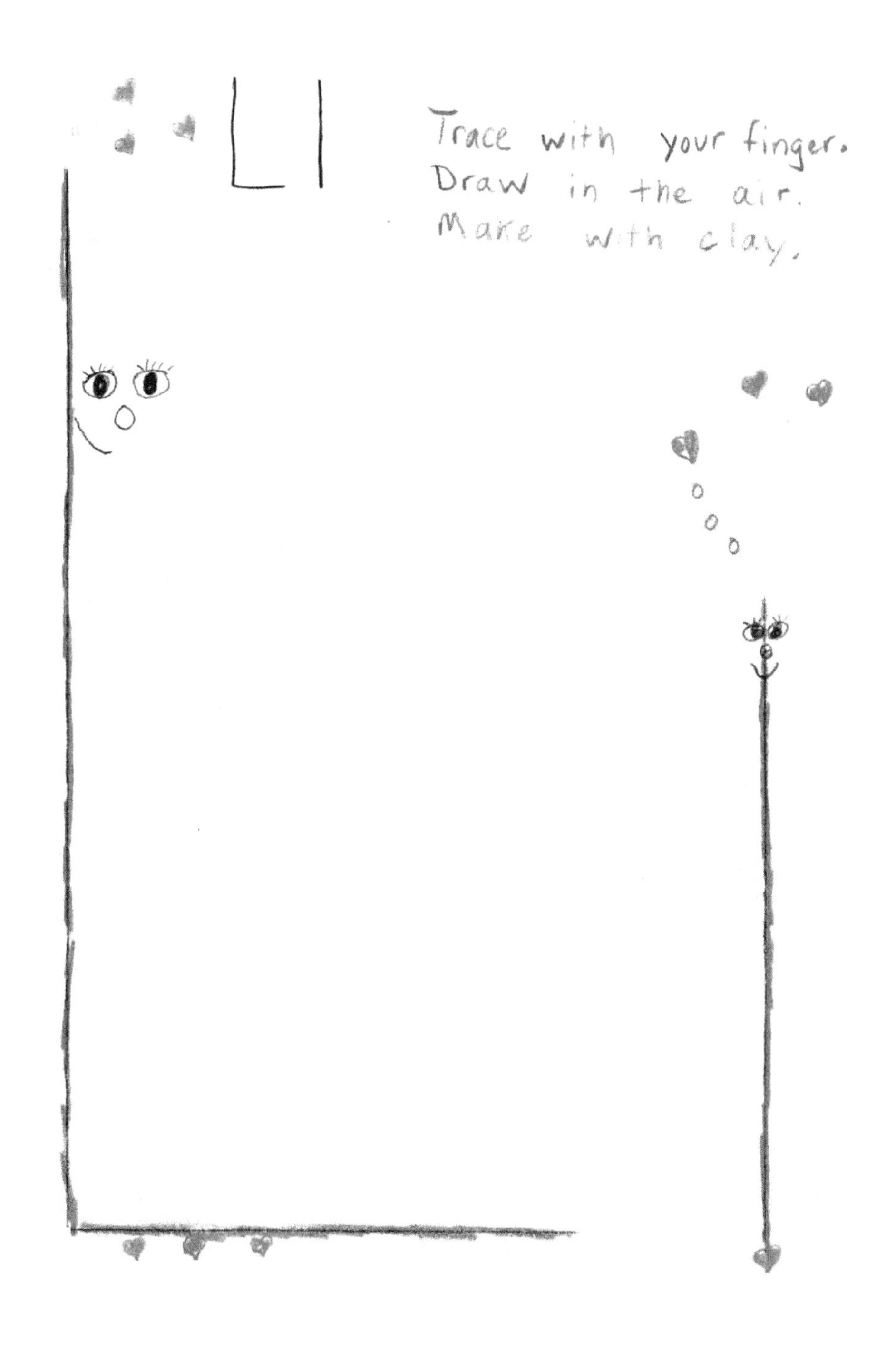
Ll
Trace with your finger.
Draw in the air.
Make with clay.

Letters Are Characters!©

About the American Reading Crisis

You are your children's first and most important teacher. You are their advocate and their support too. As such, you need to be empowered with knowledge. Collectively parents/caregivers have the power to create change, and we need to harness that power to overcome the reading crisis we are faced with today. We need to have one voice in support of best practices in reading instruction so our children can reach their highest potential and get early intervention if they need it.

The Reading Methods in Our Schools

1. The "whole-language" approach to reading instruction does not break down language into its parts and presumes that children will implicitly grasp these concepts by exposure to literature. Research has demonstrated that this is not the best way to teach our children, yet this method is still being used. In general, research takes twenty or more years to get into practice in our schools. This is a complex problem that requires changes in teacher education, staffing, and curriculum. While we wait for it to be worked out, students first need to fail to read before they get the reading intervention they need. This can close a valuable window of opportunity. If intervention is done in kindergarten, for the majority, it takes thirty minutes a day and 100 days to a year to overcome obstacles to fluency. If we wait until age nine, to achieve the same level of success, it takes two hours a day and more than a year. Most importantly, if children receive intervention at ages five and six, they may never experience the painful failure process that can leave them with lingering feelings of shame. If you hear things like "don't tell your child to sound out a word," know that this is not best practice. All children need to learn phonics and the explicit rules of spelling to

reach their highest potential as readers. (For a full historical perspective on this issue, see *Straight Talk about Learning to Read* by Hall and Moats.)

2. Phonics and explicit instruction (science based) teach children to sound out words after they learn speech sounds and letters. Children taught this way do better when reading words, spelling, and comprehending. The following are essential for optimal reading instruction:

- Speech sound/phonological awareness
- Letter recognition
- Sound-symbol correspondence
- Advanced word attack
- Sight vocabulary
- Fluent reading of text
- Spelling
- Understanding the language in books (words, sentences, paragraphs)
- Written composition
- Listening and speaking

The whole-language method was adopted without any critical evaluation of effectiveness as compared to other evidence-based approaches.

When a child is five or six, you, the parent, can spend thirty minutes a day wiring their brains for reading and building foundational reading skills that will help them succeed in school and in life. Make it your special time together. Simultaneously, we can call for systematic changes in how reading is taught in our schools.

See https://www.apmreports.org/story/2018/09/10/hard-words-why-american-kids-arent-being-taught-to-read

M is a consonant. He is a one-sound guy.

Daddy M is always hungry. He loves to m-m-munch on m-m-most anything. He eats many meals and can't fill his bumpy humps.

He says (insert *m* sound here). "Mmm, eating is so m-m-magnificient. I love m-m-muffins, m-m-meatballs, m-m-mushrooms, and m-m-milk. Actually I love food soo m-m-much. Mmm, it m-m-makes m-m-me hungry just thinking about it."

His son, baby m, m-m-mumbles because his m-m-mouth is full. "I am hungry just like m-m-my daddy. Pass the m-m-mustard greens and m-m-mac and cheese. Mmm."

Personality trait: Munchy
Favorite food: M&Ms (plain) and most anything that will fit in M's mouth.

Parent tip: Do not move on to *n* until *a*, *b*, *c*, *d*, *e*, *f*, *g*, *h*, *i*, *j*, *k*, *l*, and *m* are mastered. Play games with *a*, *b*, *c*, *d*, *e*, *f*, *g*, *h*, *i*, *j*, *k*, *l*, and *m* to review their sounds.

You are halfway through the alphabet now! Play a game with large foam or paper cutout letters. Ask your little learner to line them up in *a*, *b*, *c* order. First do the grown-ups, and then ask your learner to match the babies to their parents. Review the sound as you go.

Your learner should be able to make the letters over the forms, beside the letter forms and independently. Try writing the letters. Take your time!

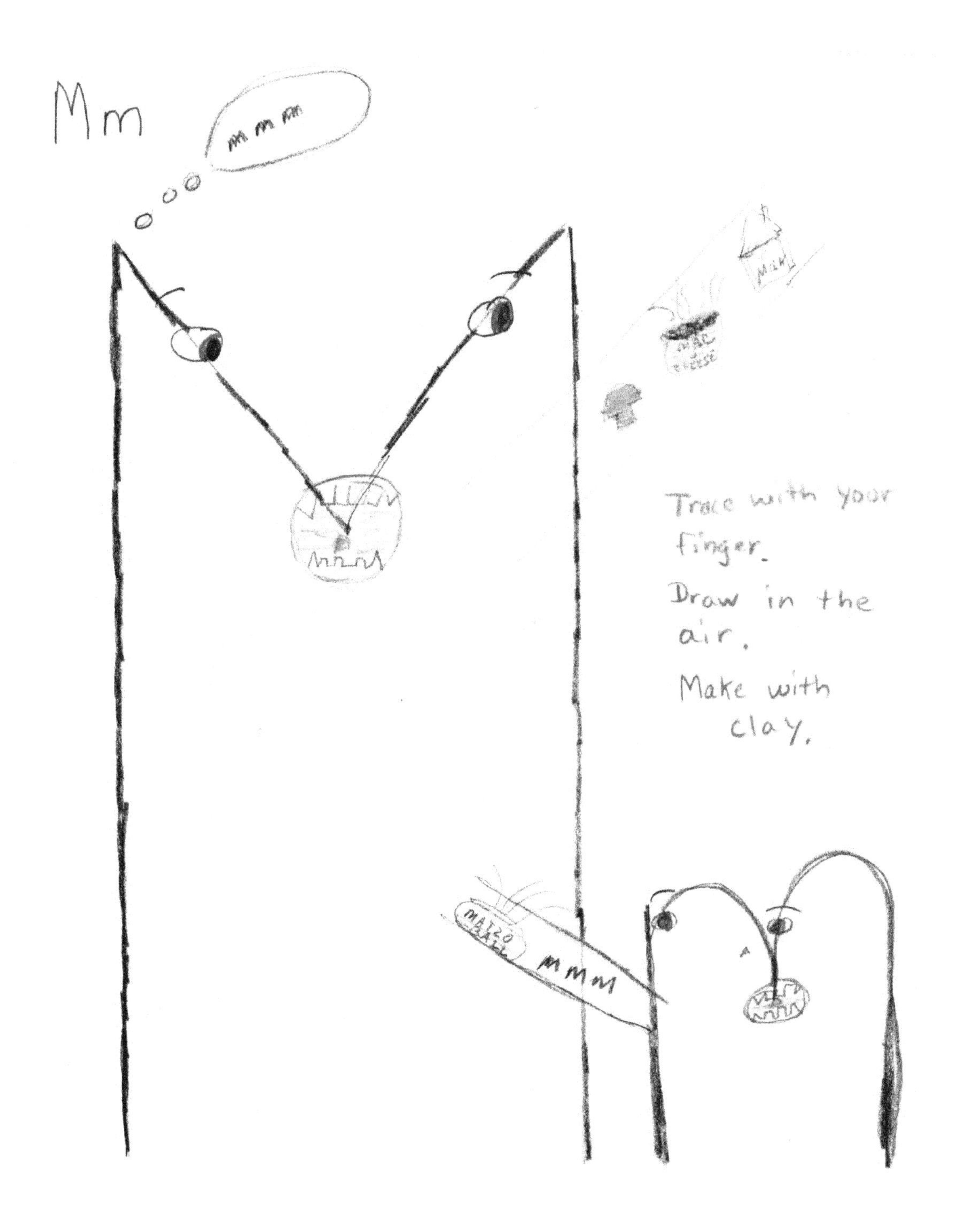

Mm
MMM
Trace with your finger.
Draw in the air.
Make with clay.

N is a consonant. She is a one-sound gal.

Mommy N always says no! She is not nice.

She says (insert *n* sound here). "N-n-noooo, I won't do this; I won't do that. I don't want this; I don't want that. You can't do this, and you can't do that. Just sit and do n-n-nothing, and don't make any n-n-noise. N-n-nobody can come over."

Her baby daughter n says no, no, no too and finds n-n-nothing is any good. When a friendly baby letter asks her to share, she crinkles up n-n-nose and makes a n-n-nasty expression and screams, "Nooooooo!" until her little baby n face turns red.

Personality trait: Negative
Favorite food: Nothing. She doesn't like anything! She'll eat nasty nuggets if she is hungry.

Parent tip: Do not move on to *o* until *a, b, c, d, e, f, g, h, i, j, k, l, m,* and *n* are mastered. Play games with *a, b, c, d, e, f, g, h, i, j, k, l, m,* and *n* to review their sounds.

Try writing the characters up to *n*, capitals and lowercase. Talk about the formation of M and N and *m* and *n*. Compare the letters.

Make a team of the bad guys. See if your child can remember.

Your learner should be able to make the letters over the forms, beside the letter forms, and independently. Try writing the letters. Take your time!

Nn

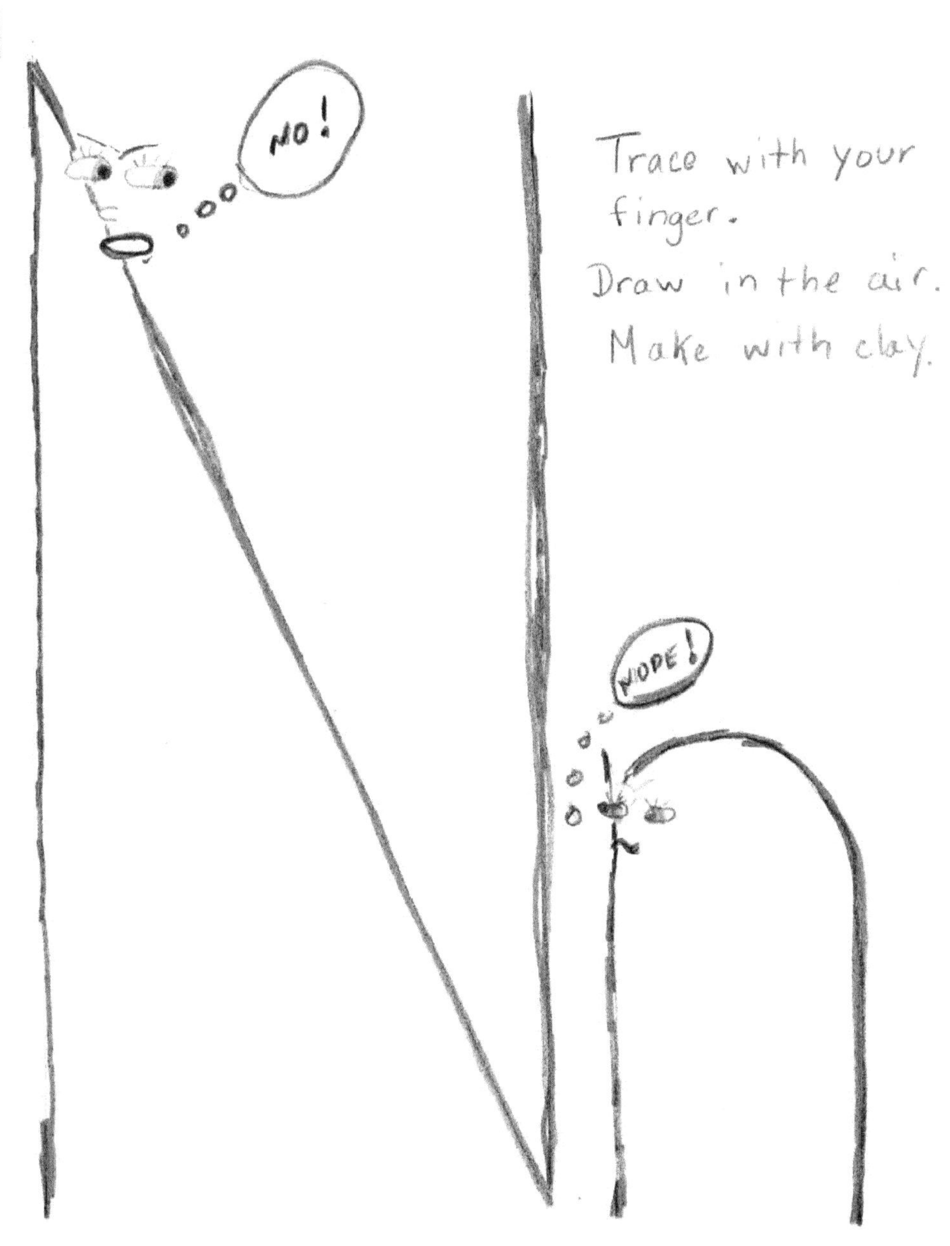

O is a vowel. He is a two-sound guy.

Daddy O is as generous as they come. Giving gifts and getting gifts is his favorite thing.

He says (insert sounds here—ō as in *Oh* and ŏ as in *ostrich*). "Oh, Oh, Oh, you have a gift for me. Aw (short *o* sound), you shouldn't have! But I am so glad that you did! Oh, I have a gift for you too; aw (*o*), I hope you like it. It is a toy o-o-ostrich named o-o-ollie!""

His baby son o, the giver of the gift, rolls around and happily says oh and aw (*o*) as he watches his dad. "Oh, I want to be just like you, Daddy."

Personality trait: Open
Favorite food: Oatmeal for breakfast and octopus on special occasions.

Parent tip: Do not move on to *p* until *a*, *b*, *c*, *d*, *e*, *f*, *g*, *h i*, *j*, *k*, *l*, *m*, *n*, and *o* are mastered. Play games with *a*, *b*, *c*, *d*, *e*, *f*, *g*, *h*, *i*, *j*, *k*, *l*, *m*, *n*, and *o* to review their sounds.

Have a letter like L give *o* a present, and practice making his sounds. Make an O shape with your mouth as you say his long sound. Compare the shape of your mouth when you say the long and short sounds.

Your learner should be able to make the letters over the forms, beside the letter forms, and independently. Try writing the letters. Take your time!

Note: Aw was added to the pronounciation of short o because it is a tricky one to articulate corrrectly even for adults.

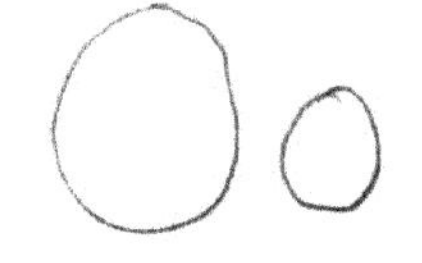

Trace with your finger.
Draw in the air.
Make with clay.

O is a vowel.

Vowels are the letters that stick words together.

All vowels are multicolored because they do lots of jobs and make more than one sound.

Letters Are Characters!©

MORPHOLOGY

IN LINGUISTICS, MORPHOLOGY is the study of the internal structure of words as they relate to meaning. This includes root woods, prefixes and suffixes, parts of speech, and more. It sounds complicated, but it isn't. In the word *morphology*, think of the suffix *ology*, which means "the study of" and was borrowed from the ancient Greeks, and the root word *morph*, which means "shape or change" and is also borrowed from Greek. The root morph and the suffix ology are used in many different words, and if your readers recognize them, they will have better comprehension and also develop richer vocabularies.

Explicit teaching of morphology to emerging readers can be done when you read aloud to them. Point out prefixes, and explain what they mean (*re*, *un*, *dis*). Point out suffixes (*s*, *es*, *ed*, *able*). Try to play games with them. Ask them if they can figure out what a word means using morphemes. (Morphemes are the smallest units of language that have meaning. Morphemic analysis is a strategy we can use to study the morphemes to determine meanings.)

For example, ask your little reader to explain the difference between the words *happy* and *unhappy*, *satisfied* and *dissatisfied*. Ask them if they can think of other little parts of words that might have meaning. What does *s* do at the end of a word? Show them a stuffed animal and stuffed animals. (Write the word *animal* beside one animal. Then add an *s* and drop in a bunch of animals beside the first animal. Make it fun!)

Working on this also helps with reading (decoding) and spelling (encoding).

Morphology instruction can be taught right along with the phonemic awareness and phonics you are doing.

How to Teach Morphology

Use hands-on activities that encourage wordplay. Get your little one moving. For example, have them shake their heads no when they see the prefix *un* or *dis*. Make something fun plural like changing *candy* to *candies*.

Here are some examples:

Root	**Meaning**	**Key Words**
rupt	to break	erupt
ject	to throw	eject
port	to carry	portable
struct	to build	construction

The prefix *e* means "out." *Ex* also means "out" as in *exit*.

Helpful materials:

https://www.criticalthinking.com/word-roots.html

https://dcps.duvalschools.org/cms/lib07/FL01903657/Centricity/Domain/5405/affixes%20and%20roots%20by%20grade%20level.pdf

Last tip for this lesson: It is helpful for little readers to touch the text. Have your little readers use their cute finger to follow the text as they read. This is a great way to point out morphemes too.

P is a consonant. She is a one-sound gal.

Mommy P has a pesky problem. She always seems to have to p-p-pee.

She says (insert *p* sound here). "I will have to excuse myself and skip to the loo because I have to pee as you can see by my wiggling and p-p-pacing. I like to drink p-p-pomegranate juice by the gallon, but I don't think that has anything do with my p-p-problem!"

Her baby girl p tags along beside her. She has to pee too but is wearing a diaper, so it is not a p-p-predicament. She wants to pee just like her mom when she grows up!

Personality trait: Pee-ceful!!
Favorite food: They like their food pureed in a liquid form. Peas, pineapple, and fruit punch are favorites.

Parent tip: Do not move on to *q* until *a, b, c, d, e, f, g, h, i, j, k, l, m, n, o,* and *p* are mastered. Play games with *a, b, c, d, e, f, g, h, i, j, k, l, m, n, o,* and *p* to review their sounds.

Introduce *p* to *e.* Play with what happens when *e* says his long sound next to *p* and when he says his short sound. Point out that two *e*'s say *ee* as in *pee, bee,* and *see.*

Your learner should be able to make the letters over the forms, beside the letter forms, and independently. Try writing the letters. Take your time!

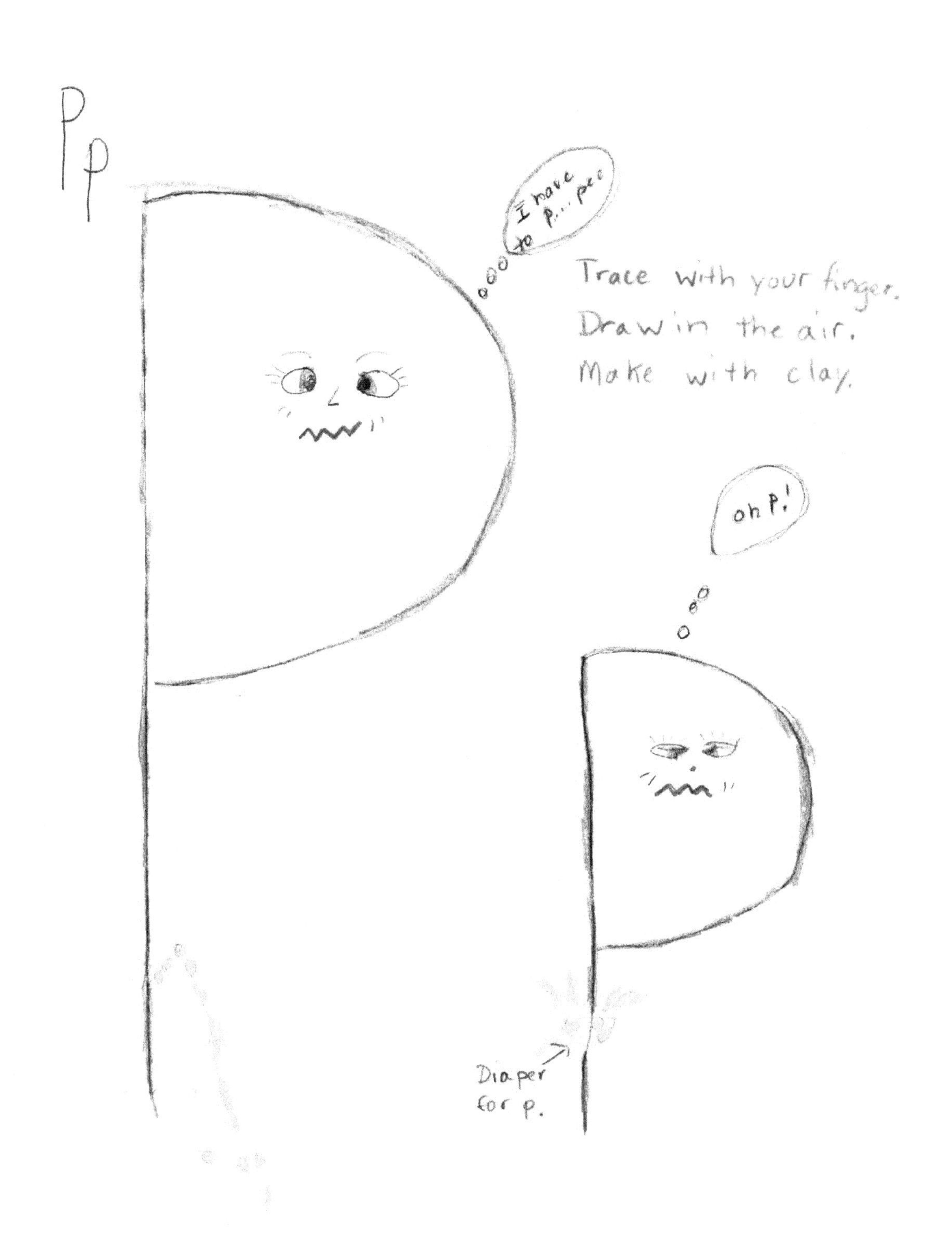
Pp
I have to p... pee
Trace with your finger.
Draw in the air.
Make with clay.
oh P!
Diaper for p.

Q is a consonant. He is a one-sound guy.

Q is good to have around if you are trying to figure something out because he always asks questions.

He says (insert the *q* [kw] sound here). "I am on a constant q-q-quest to figure things out, and the best way for me to do that is to ask q-q-quesions. Sometimes when I talk to other letters, they say, 'Stop q-q-quizzing me, Q!' But I can't stop because I am a q-q-quirky q-q-quizzer. I almost always sit beside *u*. We are best friends unquestionably."

Little baby q takes his time and says, "Daddy, how can I be just like you?" And with that q-q-question, his daddy knows that he already is just like him.

Personality trait: Quizzical
Favorite food: Quiche (real Q's eat quiche) and quince fruit. Have you ever tried it?

Parent tip: Do not move on to *r* until *a, b, c, d, e, f, g, h, i, j, k, l, m, n, o, p,* and *q* are mastered. Play games with *a, b, c, d, e, f, g, h, i, j, k, l, m, n, o, p,* and *q* to review their sounds.

Tell your little learner that *q* and *u* are best friends. They are almost always together. Write words that start with qu to show your learner. Technically q had two sounds, sometimes just sounding like k as in antique and quay. This is rare and was omitted to avoid confusion at this early stage of learning.

Your learner should be able to make the letters over the forms, beside the letter forms, and independently. Try writing the letters. Take your time!

Qq – Q's best friend is U. They are almost always together!

R is a consonant. She is a one-sound gal.

R is ready for anything. She is really, really raring to go! In her pockets she keeps everything but the kitchen sink, so she is ready to react!

She says (insert *r* sound here). "I am r-r-ready for anything. You need a r-r-rocking horse. Check! Or a r-r-rubber boot. Check! Or a r-r-rabbit? I've got you covered."

Little baby r stuffs things in her pockets and says, "Mommy, I am r-r-really r-r-ready for anything, and someday I'll be just like you."

Personality trait: Ready and raring to go
Favorite food: Radishes…wait, those are for her rabbit. Raspberries.

Parent tip: Do not move on to *s* until *a, b, c, d, e, f, g, h, i, j, k, l, m, n, o, p, q*, and *r* are mastered. Play games with *a, b, c, d, e, f, g, h, i, j, k, l, m, n, o, p, q*, and *r* to review their sounds.

Now is a good time to talk about letter blends with your little learner. Some consonants like to blend together to make sounds in words. Try putting *b* and *r* together. Shiver when you show the sound brrrr. Do the same with *d* and *r* and *p* and *r*. Explain how the letter blends bring two sounds together. Use your hands: hold up one hand and say the *b* sound; hold up the other and say the *r* sound. Clap them together and say "br."

Your learner should be able to make the letters over the forms, beside the letter forms, and independently. Try writing the letters. Take your time!

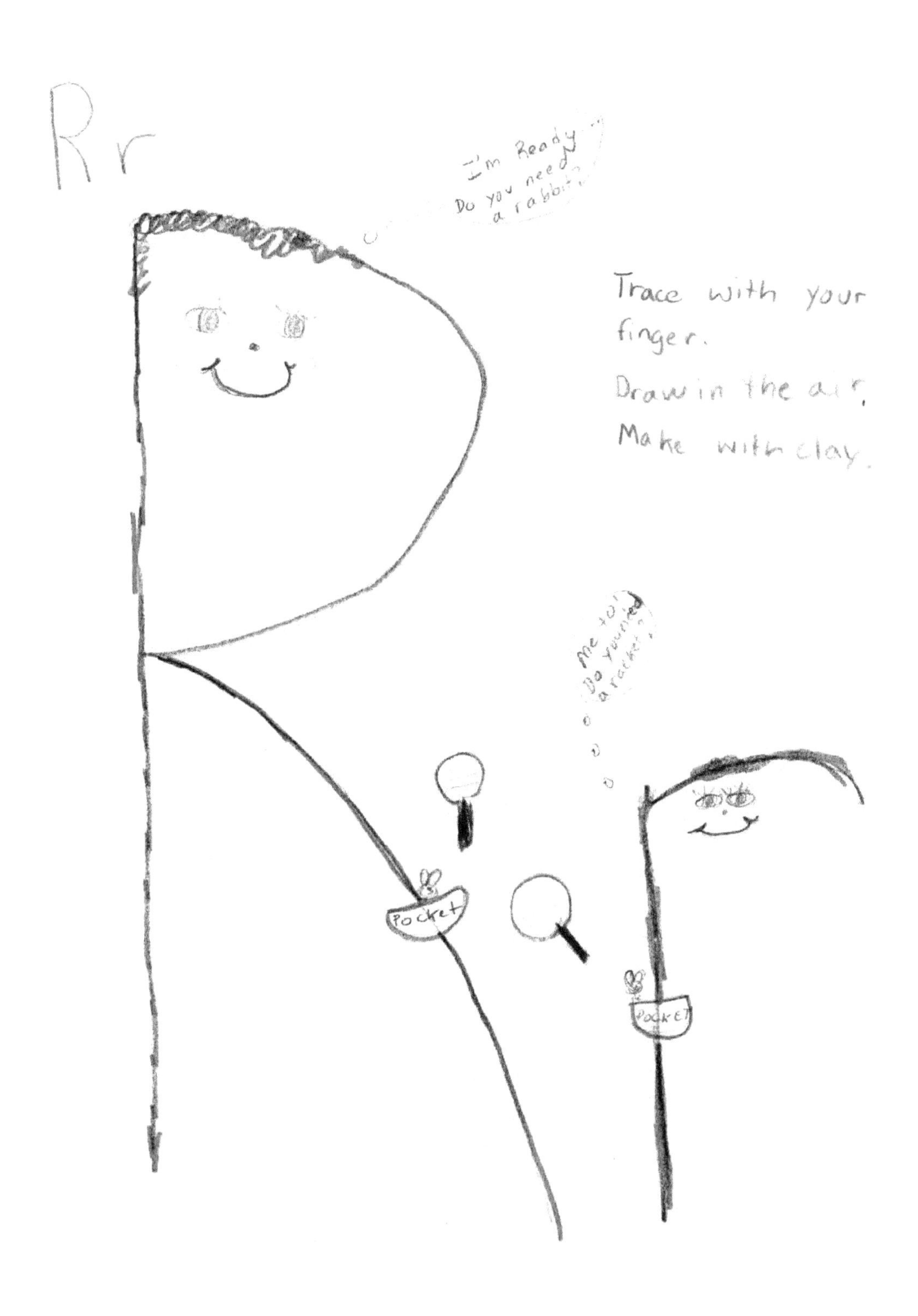
Rr
I'm Ready... Do you need a rabbit?
Trace with your finger.
Draw in the air.
Make with clay.
Me to!
Pocket
Pocket

Letters Are Characters!©

Sight Words

For our little readers, decoding and wiring their brains for reading is hard work and can be tiring. In addition to the teaching tips and strategies mentioned previously, one thing that can really help them feel confident as they learn is teaching them sight words, also known as high-frequency words. These are words that make up a large percentage (up to 75 percent) of beginning books for children. Knowing these words helps them to focus on decoding unfamiliar words and to feel the sense of accomplishment as they read. If children need to decode every single word in the text, they lose comprehension of the story and become fatigued from the effort. Additionally some sight words do not follow common letter pattern/phonics rules and cannot be easily sounded out, so teaching them can help avoid confusion.

There are several effective ways to teach sight words. Here are a few ways that you can experiment with:

1. Write the sight word on an 8½-by-11-inch piece of paper (one word per paper). Underneath the word draw an arrow. First you say the word while using the index finger and pointer of the hand that you write with to trace the line in the direction of the arrow below the word. Next have your child do the same. Repeat this see-and-say exercise.

2. Next try spell reading. Do exercise number one above and add this step: ask your little reader to spell the word after they say it. For example, have them say "the" as they underline with their fingers. Next they say "t-h-e" as they underline the words with their fingers.

3. Arm tapping. Have your child place the hand that they write with on their opposite shoulder. Then have them pat their shoulder as they say the word. Next, with their index and pointer finger, have them tap the letters of the word down their arm. Finally, have them say the word as they rub from their shoulder to their wrist with their palm.

4. Use the same paper, and have your child air-write the word as they say it.

5. Have your child trace the letters with the pointer and index finger of their writing hand on a table as they look at the word on the sheet and then underline it. Now remove the paper, and have them do it without looking at the word.

For a demonstration of the aforementioned techniques, visit,
https://sightwords.com/sight-words/lessons/air-writing/.

These techniques assist in learning because they provide kinesthetic feedback. Tapping helps because there are sensory neurons in fingertips that talk to the language parts of the brain.

You can also have children form words with clay, write them in sand, and sing their letters and sight words to help memorize them. Here is a list of sight words to get you started: a, am, an, and, are, at, can, do, for, go, has, have, he, here, I, in, is, it, like, look, me, my, no, play, said, see, she, so, the, to, up, and we.

For a full list of sight words, Google Dolch words, or high-frequency words, visit https://sightwords.com/sight-words/dolch/#lists. Many great lists are available.

S is a consonant. He is a two-sound guy (/*s*/ and /*z*/ as in *bees*).
He says (insert *s* and *z* sounds here).

S is s-s-super, s-s-silly, and s-s-smart. He has some s-s-special magical powers. If you add him to the end of the word, he makes it more. When he does this, sometimes he sounds like a *z*, especially if the word ends in a vowel like *flies*. He likes to make more of really s-s-sweet things like if you have a s-s-smile, put him at the end, and you have *smiles-s-s*!

"I want you to know that s-s-snakes are s-s-super. Yes-s-s, I s-s-slither. I even s-s-sometimes s-s-slide! I am s-s-so s-s-swell."

S-s-suddenly baby s s-s-shows up and s-s-says, "I s-s-snuck! I nearly got s-s-stuck, but I s-s-slipped through. I want to be s-s-super like you, Dad."

Personality trait: Smiley
Favorite food: Slushies with strawberries

Parent tip: Do not move on to *t* until *a, b, c, d, e, f, g, h, i, j, k, l, m, n, o, p, q, r*, and *s* are mastered. Play games with *a, b, c, d, e, f, g, h, i, j, k, l, m, n, o, p, q, r*, and *s* to review their sounds.

Take a word like *cat*. Add an *s* and show how you would have more than one cat with *s*! Use objects to demonstrate this, or draw a cat; then add an *s* and show that you have *cats*. Now is a good time to play a game with large foam letters in which you ask your reader to match the baby letter with the daddy letter. Also spend some time with your little one and practice tracing them over paper cutouts of letters.

Your learner should be able to make the letters over the forms, beside the letter forms, and independently. Try writing the letters. Take your time!

Ss

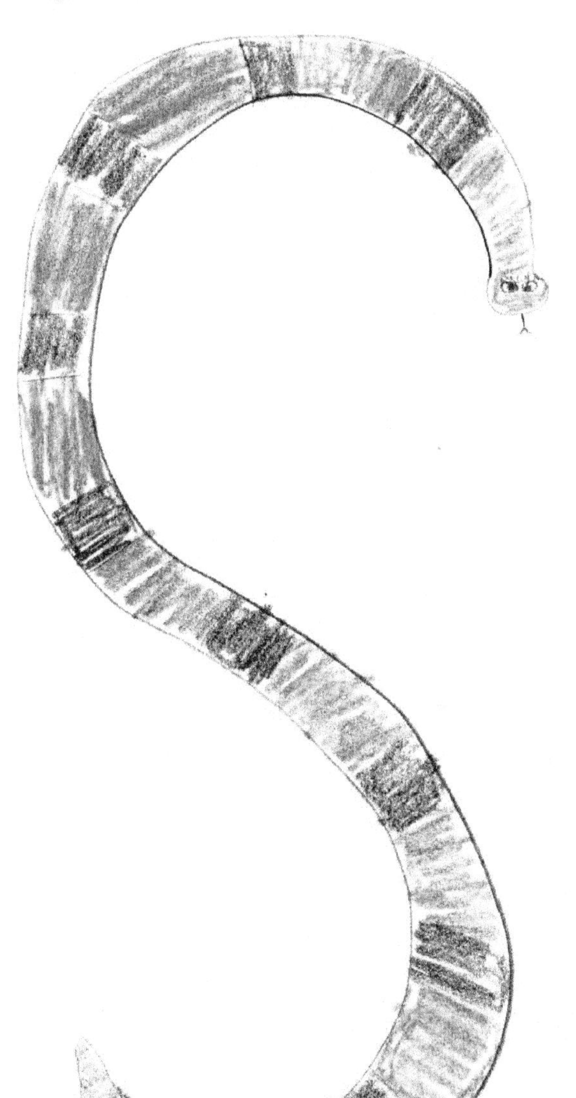

Trace with your finger.

Draw in the air.

Make with clay.

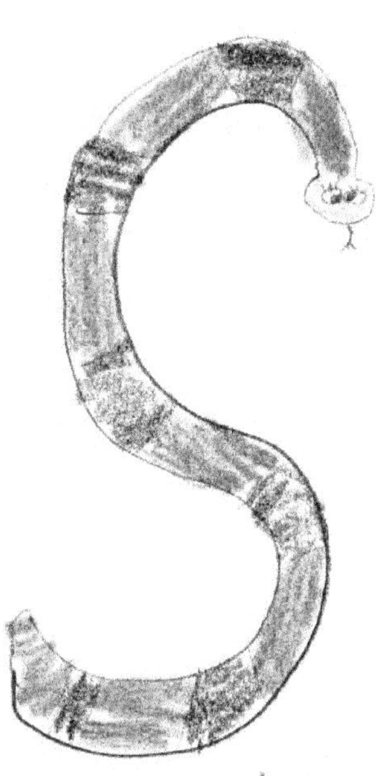

S has two sounds so he has two colors.

T is a consonant. She is a one-sound gal.

T has t-t-trouble. She t-t-teeters and t-t-totters and t-t-tips. Woo-hoo, there she goes now!

She says (insert *t* sound here). "Be careful, my big t-t-top makes me t-t-tip. But when I stand beside a letter friend, it holds me up so I don't t-t-topple."

T-t-tiny t is not as t-t-tippy. She tips for fun as she says, "Being a t-t-tipper t-t-topper is t-t-teriffic!"

Personality trait: Tip-top
Favorite foods: Tater Tots with tea

Parent tip: Do not move on to *u* until *a, b, c, d, e, f, g, h, i, j, k, l, m, n, o, p, q, r, s,* and *t* are mastered. Play games with *a, b, c, d, e, f, g, h, i, j, k, l, m, n, o, p, q, r, s,* and *t* to review their sounds.

T is a great letter to use when continuing to work on blends. A consonant blend consists of two consonants that combine, but each sound can still be heard. Examples include *tr* (train), *st* (stop), and *ft* (gift). Digraphs are letter blends that combine to make one sound, but you cannot hear each individual letter sound (*ph, th, sh*).

Your learner should be able to make the letters over the forms, beside the letter forms, and independently. Try writing the letters. Take your time!

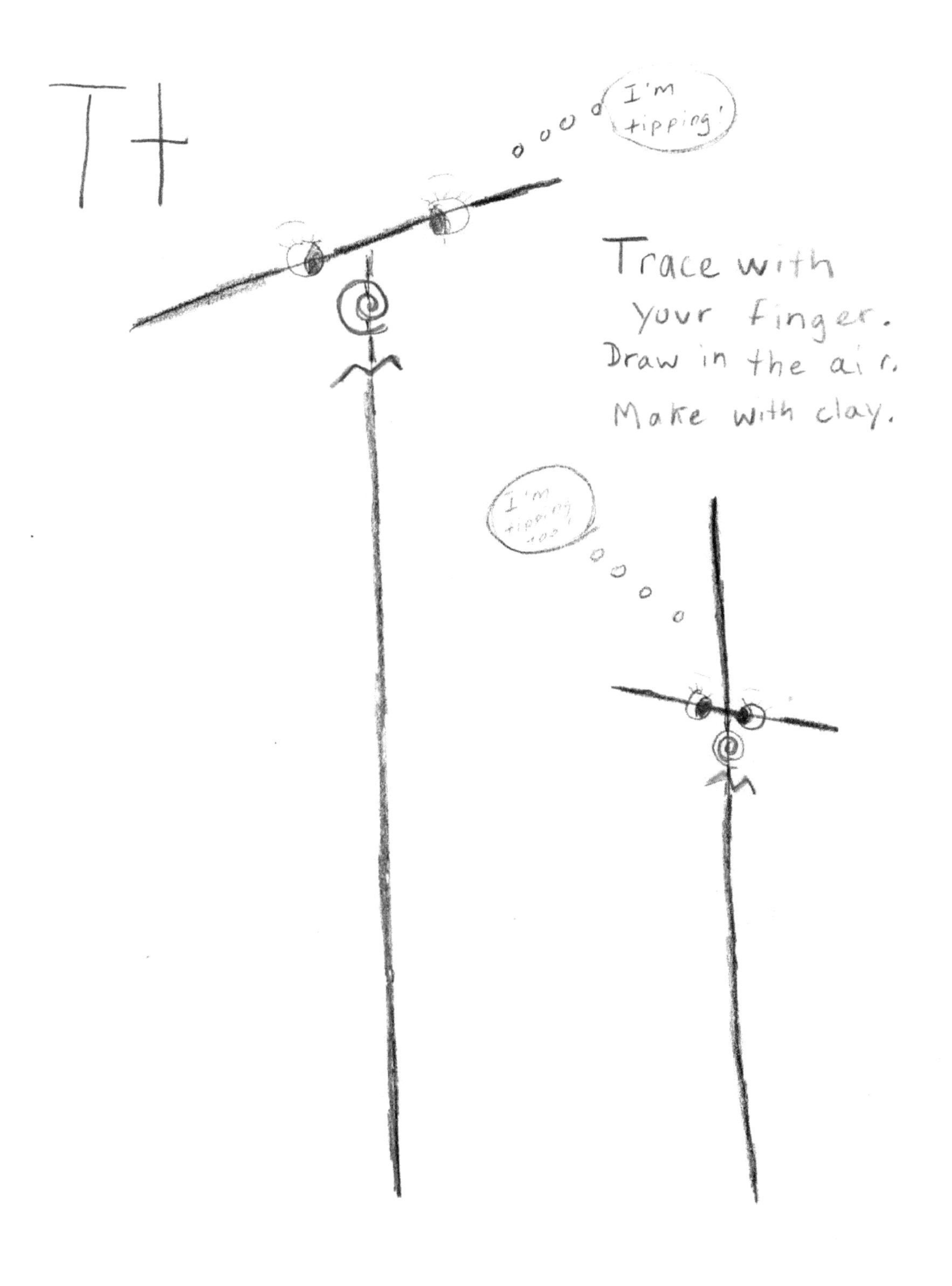
Tt
I'm tipping!
Trace with your finger.
Draw in the air.
Make with clay.
I'm

U is vowel. He is a two-sound guy.

U is u-u-utterly unselfish. He always wants to talk about you...U-U-U. He is a little shy and sometimes uses his short sound to get the conversation going. He is one of the nicest letters of all.

He says (insert two sounds here ū (U) and ŭ (u) as in umbrella). "You are u-u-unique. I want to hear all about you. What do you like to eat, u-u-umbrella fruit? What do you like for dessert, u-u-upsidedown cake? What is your favorite color? Tell me about you."

Little baby u always shares and always thinks of others too. "Daddy, tell me about you. Lift me u-u-up." He will grow up to be just like his dad, doing for others and filled with u-u-understanding.

Personality trait: Unselfish
Favorite foods: Umbrella fruit and Upside-Down Cake

Parent tip: Do not move on to *v* until *a, b, c, d, e, f, g, h, i, j, k, l, m, n, o, p, q, r, s, t,* and *u* are mastered. Play games with *a, b, c, d, e, f, g, h, i, j, k, l, m, n, o, p, q, r, s, t,* and *u* to review their sounds.

Now it is time to put out all the vowels. Explain that vowels are words that stick letters together. Take the word c-u-p. Say each sound and blend them together. Teach your reader that when *e* sits at the end of a consonant-vowel-consonant word, he makes the first vowel brave, and he stays silent (*cap* to *cape, bat* to *bate, mat* to *mate*, etc.).

Your learner should be able to make the letters over the forms, beside the letter forms, and independently. Try writing the letters. Take your time!

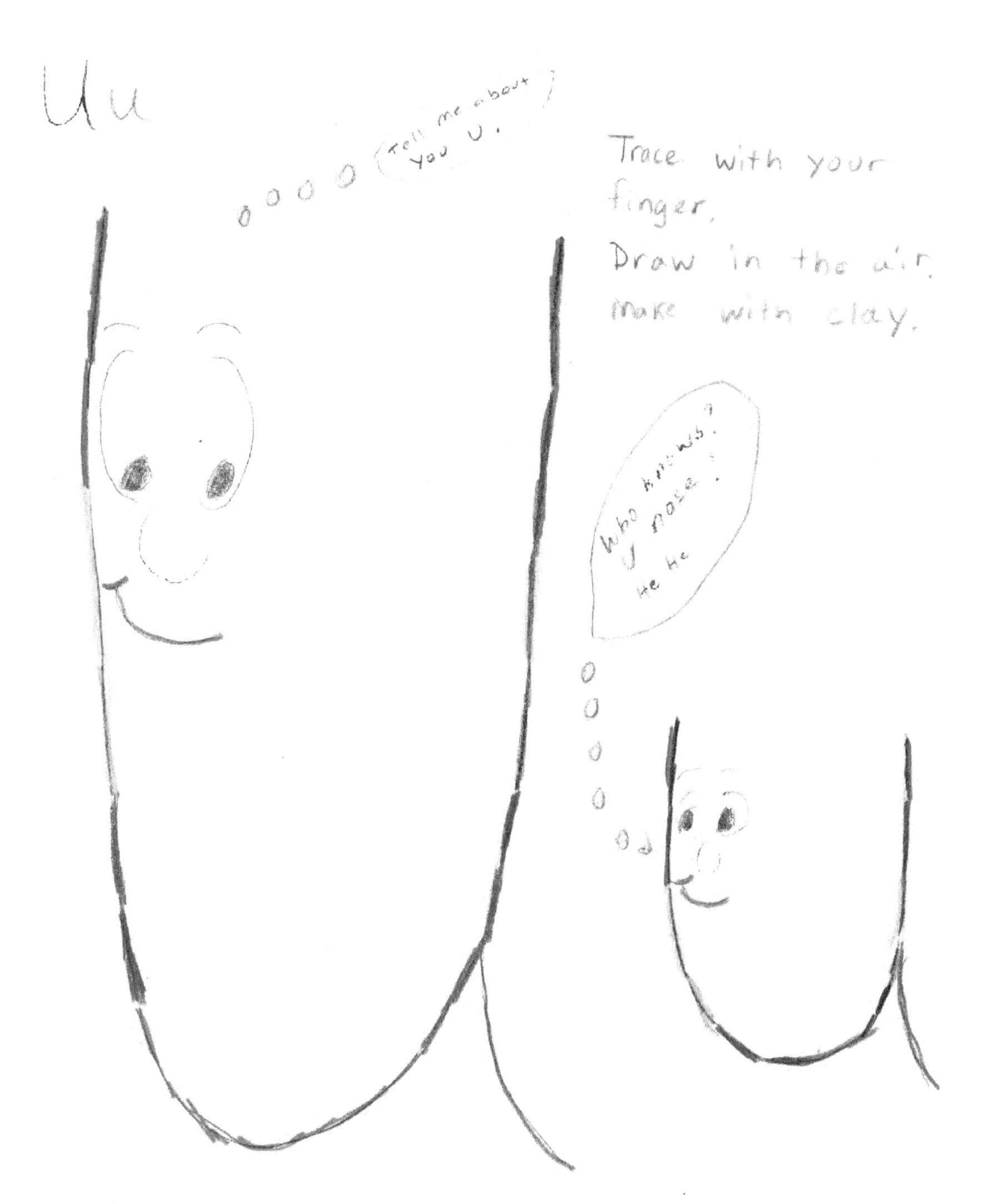

All vowels are multicolored because they do lots of jobs and make more than one sound!

Letters Are Characters!©

Writing Letters, Pictures in the Text, and Other Caregiver Coaching Tips

On Writing

We are almost at the end of the alphabet. Your readers may be getting close to cracking the phonemic code. When they do this, it is one of the most exciting moments for you, their first and most invested teacher. You did it. You started them on the road to literacy. They may begin saying the letters and their sounds automatically now. They are likely ready to try their hand at writing them if they have not already. At some point, when they seem to be drawn to drawing, make an event of presenting them with their very own pencils and workbooks. *Handwriting without Tears* offers explicit handwriting instruction (https://www.lwtears.com/hwt). Children who get comfortable with handwriting are better able to express their ideas as they begin writing.

Practice writing the letters with your child, and see if you can draw their faces and remember their personalities and what they say. The illustrations are simple so children can draw them by copying the lines. Have fun. Make games with *b* and *d* and B and D. And then let p play; b, d, and p are difficult for many children. Other tricky ones might be V, v, and W, w, which can also confuse our little ones, as well as M, m, and N, n. Find tricks that will help little ones see the differences. Pay attention to where they get confused with recognizing and naming the character, attaching the sound, and writing, and create lessons accordingly. This will make them feel so much more comfortable in a classroom setting where teachers cannot give individualized instruction to the extent that you can.

Beginning to Sound Out and Read Automatically

After your reader has cracked the phonemic code, they will begin decoding. Simultaneously they will begin to recognize some sight words. *They are reading!* This is a great time to pick up some short, simple books or make your own with beginner words. Bob books are great because they contain just the right amount of words to decode and sight read.

(Visit https://www.bobbooks.com/.)

If they struggle with a word in the text, do not rush them by supplying it. Give them time. Children are much more patient than adults. If they are getting frustrated, supply the word for them by first sounding it out. If it is an unfamiliar letter combination (like *knob* or *phone*), just read it to them until they are ready for learning that level of complexity. Children should not guess at words by using pictures or context, as they are trying to learn to decode, which involves recognizing letter patterns. Guessing does not help in this regard and is usually inaccurate. Pictures should only be used to confirm that they have sounded out the word properly. For some little ones, pictures are very distracting and make them lose focus. If this is happening, write a simple sentence on a large piece of paper. Then, after they have decoded it with you, show them the picture or test comprehension by drawing one together.

Correcting your child's reading errors must be done gently and carefully so as not to discourage your little ones. Let some mistakes go, and revisit them if your child seems to be in flow with their reading. Or gently ask them to try again, and do it with them if they are getting frustrated.

When reading a book together, take time to review the cover, pointing out the title of the book and the author's name. Encourage your reader to use his or her finger to follow along with the text.

At some point after we read a word enough times, we stop decoding it and process it automatically. This takes time (four to fifteen times for an average reader and up to forty for a struggling reader). The journey to fluency is different for everyone because every brain is unique.

V is a consonant. She is a one-sound gal.

V wants to win. The taste of v-v-victory is sweet on her v-v-vicious tongue. However, she is a v-v-very bad sport, and this makes her a v-v-villain.

She says (insert *v* sound here). "I am v-v-very v-v-vocal about my v-v-victories, and I use my v-v-voice to say, 'I win, you lose.' Being a good sport is v-v-vulgar!"

Little v pushes past her mom. "V-v-vroom, Mommy, I won that race. You lose." Baby v wants to be just like her mom.

Personality trait: Vicious
Favorite foods: Victorious veggies (Only blue-ribbon prize winners will do!)

Parent tip: Do not move on to *w* until *a, b, c, d, e, f, g, h, i, j, k, l, m, n, o, p, q, r, s, t, u*, and *v* are mastered. Play games with *a, b, c, d, e, f, g, h, i, j, k, l, m, n, o, p, q, r, s, t, u*, and *v* to review their sounds.

To help your learner remember V, which is often confused with W, hold up your two arms in a V and say, "Victory." Pretend that V is in a race with another letter and act out their parts.

Your learner should be able to make the letters over the forms, beside the letter forms, and independently. Try writing the letters. Take your time!

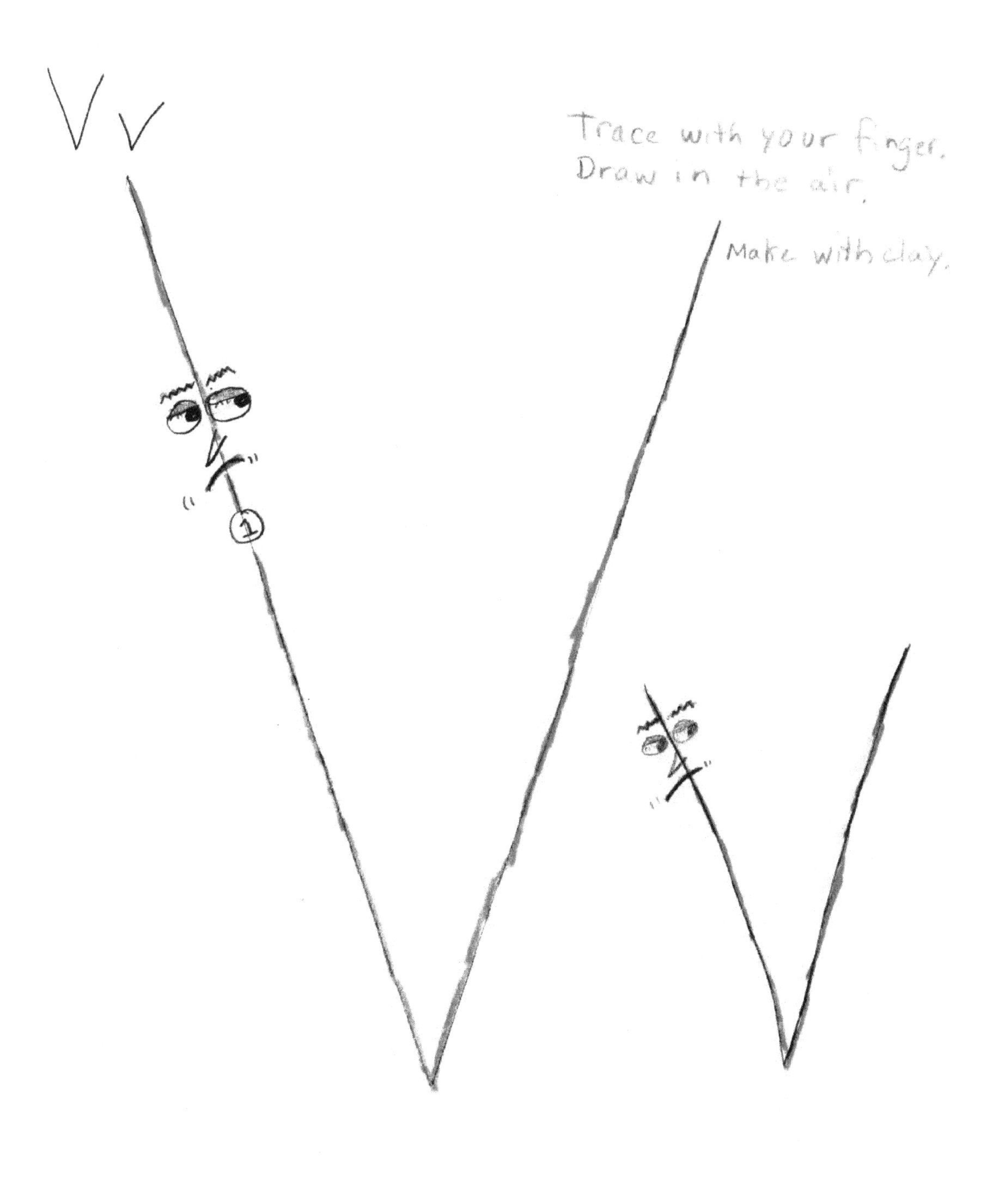
Vv
Trace with your finger.
Draw in the air.
Make with clay.
1

W is a consonant. He is a one-sound guy.

W can't stay still. He w-w-wiggles and w-w-waggles and w-w-wobbles all around. It is his w-w-way

"W-w-wooo, w-w-watch out. I am w-w-wiggling and w-w-waggling out of control. I am going to w-w-wobble off the page. It is sort of fun."

Little baby w, only a toddler, w-w-watches. "W-w-wiggling and w-w-wobbling are w-w-wonderful, Dad. I love being a *w*."

Personality trait: Wonderful and wobbly
Favorite foods: Watermelon and wiggly worms

Parent tip: Do not move on to *v* until *a*, *b*, *c*, *d*, *e*, *f*, *g*, *h*, *i*, *j*, *k*, *l*, *m*, *n*, *o*, *p*, *q*, *r*, *s*, *t*, *u*, *v*, and *w* are mastered. Play games with *a*, *b*, *c*, *d*, *e*, *f*, *g*, *h*, *i*, *j*, *k*, *l*, *m*, *n*, *o*, *p*, *q*, *r*, *s*, *t*, *u*, *v*, and *w* to review their sounds.

Play with the wiggly *w*'s. Ask them to w-w-wait. They can't; they must wiggle. Ask your little one to wiggle with *w*! Put on some music, and do the *w* wiggle.

Your learner should be able to make the letters over the forms, beside the letter forms, and independently. Try writing the letters. Take your time!

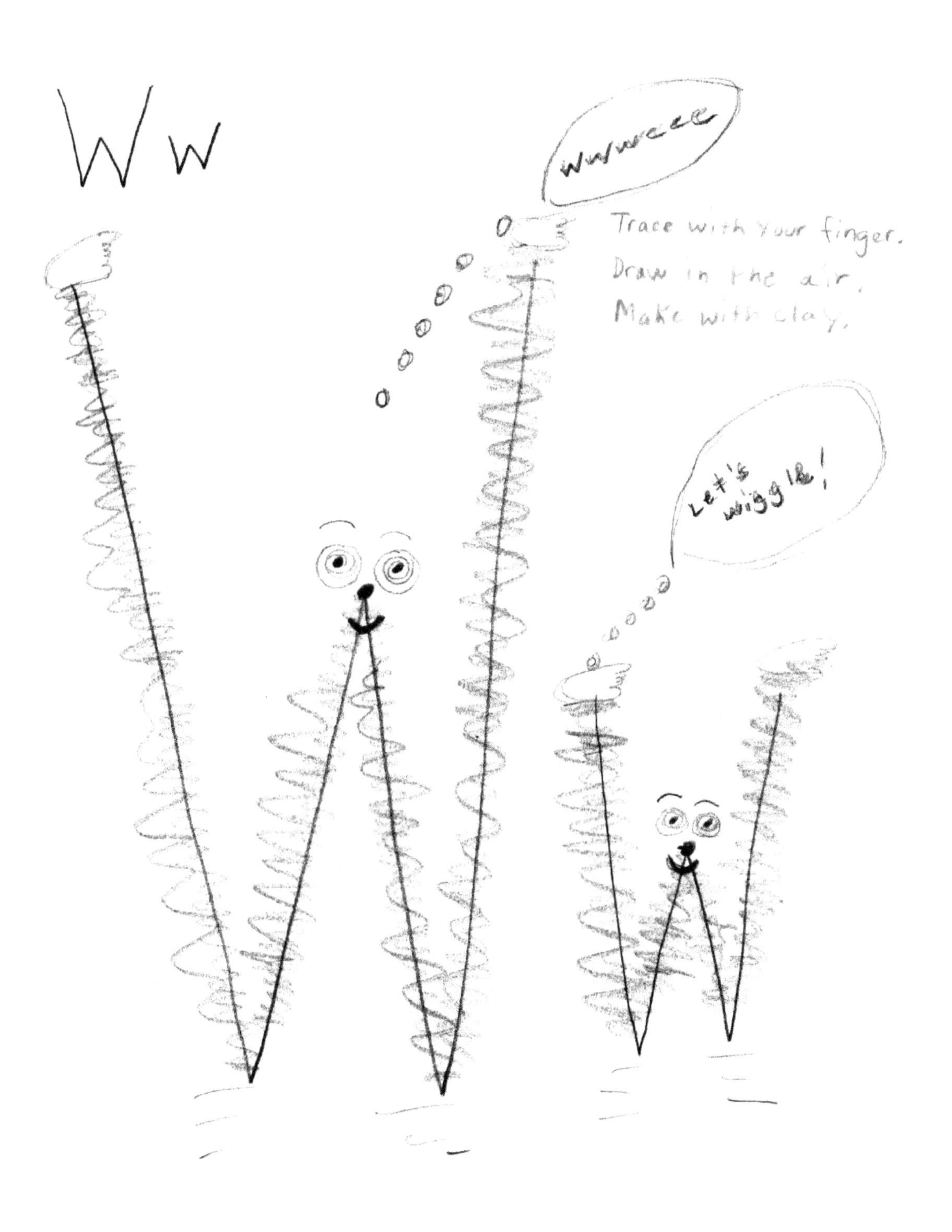
Ww
wwweee
Trace with your finger.
Draw in the air.
Make with clay.
Let's wiggle!

X is a consonant. She can make a few sounds. (/*x*/, /*ks*/ and /*z*/)

X is a pirate letter; what she likes most is finding where she marks the spot to discover treasure. She has a secret power: X-ray vision. She can see right through the treasure chest without even using an ax (*ks* sound) to open it and tell you what's inside! She can't wait to go on her next adventure. Since she steals a lot, she has even taken sounds from other letters! She steals z's sound in words like xylophone.

She says (insert sound here, ks and x). "Argh, mates, I am Pirate X, and I love to take my *extra* treasure, my *ax,* and my friends K, S, and I out on my pirate ship to sail the seven seas."

Little baby x puts on her Captain Hook costume, hugs her mommy's leg, and says, "Argh, I want to be an extra-great pirate like you!"

Personality trait: Extraordinarily greedy
Favorite food: Not hungry. She is too busy looking for *extra* gold. She does like cookies shaped like an X.

Parent tip: Do not move on to *y* until *a, b, c, d, e, f, g, h, i, j, k, l, m, n, o, p, q, r, s, t, u, v, w,* and *x* are mastered. Play games with *a, b, c, d, e, f, g, h, i, j, k, l, m, n, o, p, q, r, s, t, u, v, w,* and *x* to review their sounds.

This might be a good time to explain to your little reader that for certain letters, where the letter is positioned in a word determines which sound they will make. Put X at the beginning of a word, and it says its name or the *z* sound (Xerox). Put *x* in the word, and it often says its *ks* sound. It sounds complex, but introduce the concept and you may find that it makes sense to your little one.

Your learner should be able to make the letters over the forms, beside the letter forms, and independently. Try writing the letters. Take your time!

Note: Although X makes three sounds, focus on two as the z cound can be confusing at this point in learning. It is good to mention this third sound early on but focus on the ks and x sounds for now. This is why the illustration has two colors instead of three.

Xx
I see inside with my Xray vision!
Trace with your finger.
Draw in the air
Make with clay.
X-RAY
VISION
Want to play jaX?
X has two sounds so
She has two colors.

Letters Are Characters!©

On Pace of Reading Acquisition and After Your Learner Cracks the Phonemic Code, On to Consonant Blends

The Rush to Read

If we rush our children to read before they are ready, we lose the joy of the journey. This process of reading acquisition, even for struggling readers, can be joyful and filled with moments of discovery, laughter, and connection.

Although reading happens in the brain and the amount of repetition needed varies from child to child based on the brain's wiring, there is a development piece that needs to be considered. Some children—particularly boys who have no areas in which they are struggling—are simply not ready to read until they are around six. Evaluation needs to be done to make sure that this is the case. Ideally, children should begin learning their letters and attaching their corresponding sounds before and during kindergarten. If they struggle, this is a red flag, and early interventions should be started. If they struggle with word finding, this is another warning sign. If they mispronounce phonemes in words (*eyeflashes* for *eyelashes*, etc.), pay attention.

This is different from starting to read. We don't want to push our children to acquire reading earlier than they are ready, as this is may cause other impediments. Ages five, six and seven seem to be an optimal times to begin reading acquisition as opposed to earlier when the focus is best placed on phonemic awareness, cracking the phonemic code, and other reading readiness skills, such as building phonological awareness, vocabulary, and comprehension skills through reading aloud.

The reading journey is like climbing steps. If our children skip steps, they can fall and are likely to miss things that are helpful.

There are five big elements that need to be in reading programs at the right time in the right measure:

1. Phonemic awareness—understanding that words are made of sounds. Phonemes are the smallest units of sounds.

2. Phonics—learning that letters correspond to sounds. This helps them sound out words (decode) and later spell them (encode). They need to learn that letters and letter patterns are predictable. Example: C says its hard sound when it sits next to *a*, *o*, or u, and it says its soft sound when it sits next to *i*, *e*, or *y*. Explicit learning is always better. (Eighty-seven percent of the English language follows the rules.)

3. Vocabulary—understanding the meaning of words and knowing how to pronounce them will help our children in many ways, including reading comprehension and fluency. Reading aloud and taking the time to check in to explain unfamiliar words is a great way to build vocabulary.

4. Reading fluency—fluency is the ability to recognize words and read them accurately without decoding them. This happens over time and requires much practice. (Again some children require upward of forty repetitions of a word before they can read it fluently; some children require only four.) Read with your children even after they seem to be fluent. Reading education often ends in our schools in fourth grade, yet most of our readers still need coaching to read with fluency.

5. Comprehension—the culmination of all of the aforementioned reading skills. Check in with your children early and often when they are reading or being read to. All of the reading skills are interrelated, so a breakdown in one area can cause problems in another. Research indicates that more than 95 percent of kids can learn to read at an average level if they are given the proper intervention, which requires targeted assessments and goals and progress monitoring.

Now, back to what to do after your child has cracked the phonemic code (understands the alphabetic principle). Review with them that when letters come together, sometimes they make two-letter blends. Use the letter characters and have them come together. (B bounces in and sits next to loving L, and together they say *Bl.*) Let's start with some consonant blends; they blend together, yet both sounds can still be heard.

Examples of Consonant Blends

Bl—as in block	Br—as in brush
Cl—as in clock	Cr—as in crab
Dr—as in drum	Fl—as in flower
Fr—as in frog	Gl—as in glue
Gr—as in grape	Pl—as in plane
Pr—as in pretzel	Sc—as in scale
Sl—as in sleep	Sk—as in skate
Sn—as in snow	Sp—as in spoon
St—as in star	Tr—as in train

Next we will move to trickier concepts. Digraphs are letters that come together and make only one sound, such as *ch*, *sh*, *ph*, *th*, *wh*, and *kn*. More on these later.

USE THIS PAGE FOR NOTES, DOODLES AND DRAWINGS

Y can be a consonant or a vowel. He is a two-sound guy.

Y is the most curious and versatile letters of all. He is always asking questions and ready to help his friends. He is unique because he can be either a vowel or a consonant. Why not Y?

He says (insert three sounds here—Y as in *yellow*, I as in *by*, and E as in *very*). "Why? Why do you need to stick to being either a vowel or a consonant when you can be both? Why? Why? Why? Y? Y? Y? I have special powers of discovery. I can figure things out. I usually say y-y-yes. I sometimes take over for *i* when *i* is too busy thinking about himself as in the words *by* and *my*. Why? I even sometimes help *e*. Yes, I am ver*y* fine."

Little baby y says, "Looky, looky, Daddy! I can make so many sounds and help the other letters just like you. My favorite color is y-y-yellow."

Personality trait: He is a yes-man!
Favorite food: Yellow squash

Parent tip: Do not move on to *z* until *a, b, c, d, e, f, g, h, i, j, k, l, m, n, o, p, q, r, s, t, u, v, w, x*, and *y* are mastered. Play games with *a, b, c, d, e, f, g, h, i, j, k, l, m, n, o, p, q, r, s, t, u, v, w, x*, and *y* to review their sounds.

Review the vowels. Sing a vowel song and add "sometimes *y*." If you have letters, get out all of the vowels, and have them play together and sing their sounds.

Your learner should be able to make the letters over the forms, beside the letter forms, and independently. Try writing the letters. Take your time!

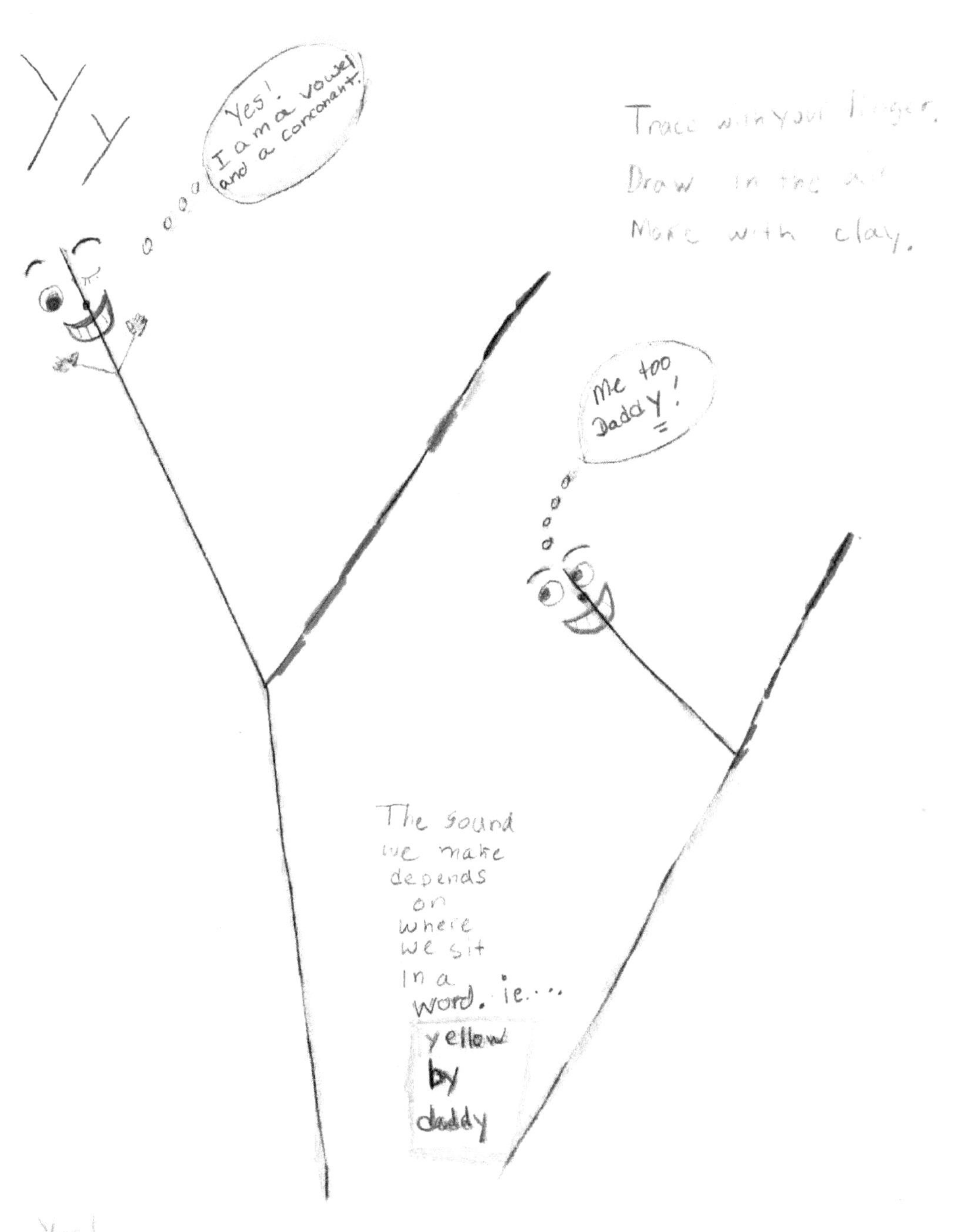
Yy
Yes! I am a vowel and a consonant.
Trace with your finger.
Draw in the air
Make with clay.
Me too Daddy Y!
The sound we make depends on where we sit in a word. ie....
yellow
by
daddy
Yes!
At the beginning of a word Y is a consonant.
If he sits anywhere else he says ī or ē.

Z is a consonant. She is a one-sound gal.

Z is the last letter in the alphabet. She is always zigging and zagging to catch up with her friends in the alphabet.

She says (insert *z* sound here). "Z-Z-Zip, z-z-zig, z-z-zag…I am a fast friend who loves to z-z-zoom."

Little baby z looks on and says, "Z-z-zig, z-z-zag, z-z-zoom, I am zippy like you, Mommy!"

Personality trait: Zippy and full of zest for Life
Favorite food: Ziti made with zucchini!

Take *Z* and have her zoom and zip around. Put her on a toy with wheels or a toy airplane!

Dear Parent/Caregiver,
Well done! You deserve to treat yourself and your learner to something special because you did it. As soon as your learners can recognize all of the letter symbols and attach their sounds, they have broken the phonemic code. Their brains are ready to learn to read. Enjoy the journey and dive into books together. Speech is learned through imitation so reading aloud helps with vocabulary. Decoding takes practice, so now that you are in the habit of teaching reading to your little one, do it a little every day. You'll never regret the time that you spend together reading, an activity that is uniquely human and profound. Reading connects us, and we need that connection to be whole through our interconnectedness. Thank you for taking this journey with the letter characters. They have loved being with you and your child.

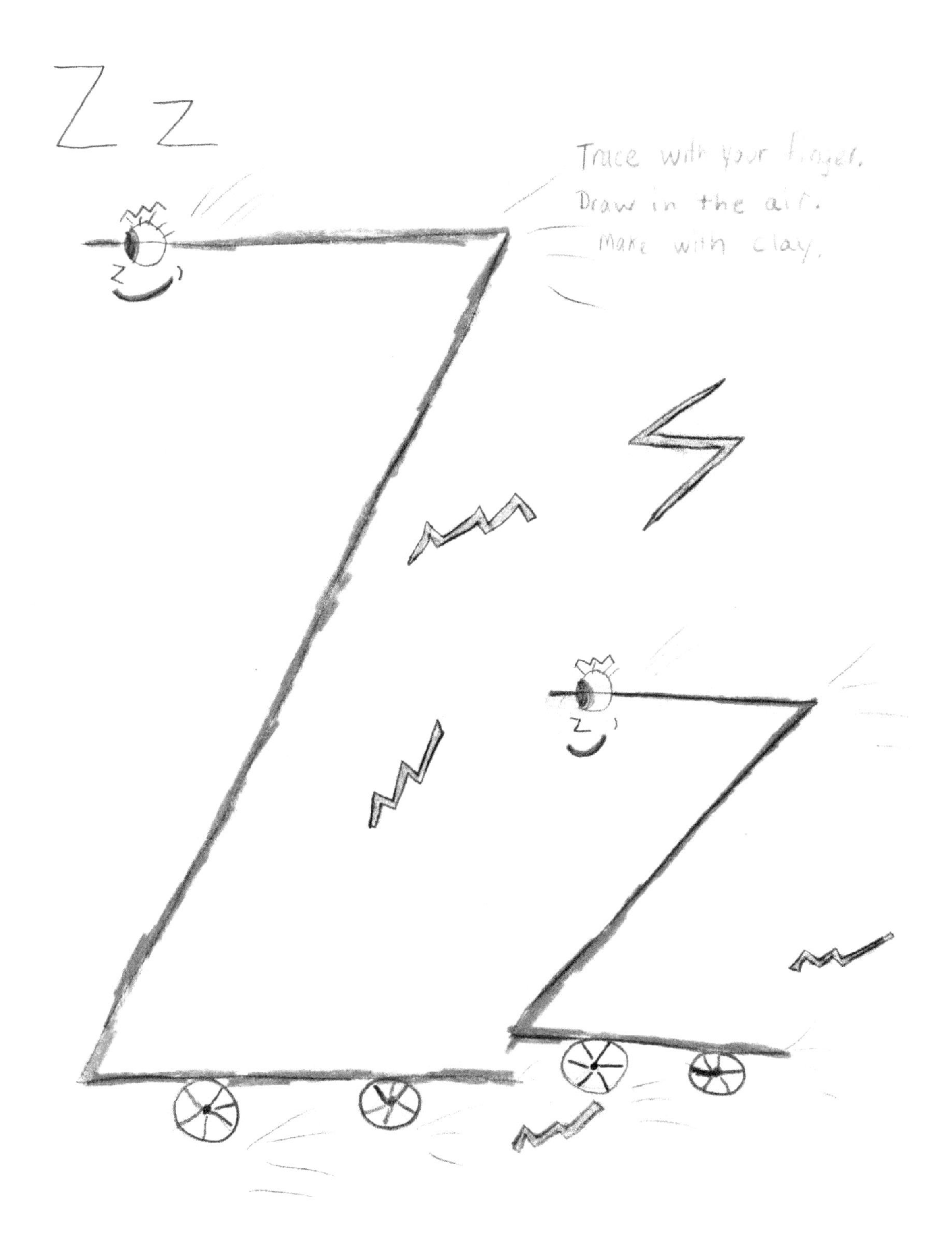
Z z
Trace with your finger.
Draw in the air.
Make with clay.

Letters Are Characters!©

Digraphs, Vowels, and School Reading Curriculum Must-Haves

Digraphs are two letters that come together and make one sound. They need to be taught explicitly. They are different from the blends discussed previously where the letter sounds can still be heard and are technically two phonemes, such as in *br* or *st*. Your learner needs to be anchored in the understanding that letters are not random and that letter patterns are predictable. They just take time to learn. More than 87 percent of words follow specific rules and have predictable letter patterns, but the rules take time to know and teach.

Digraphs can be made of vowels or consonants. Here is a list to start with:
Ch as in choo, choo (train)
Th as in Thursday
Wh as in what
Sh as in sharp
Ck (at the end of the word) as in duck
Ph as in phone
Kn as in knee

Digraphs can also be made of vowel combinations:
Ai
Ee or Ea
Ie
Oa
Ue
A fun way to explain these for a simple introduction to the concept is "in many words when two vowels go walking, the first does the talking." It is not always true—think of *oo* (as in *boo*) or *oi* (as in *oil*)—but it works in many cases and is a good way to introduce the concept.

There are more, but this is a good starting place to introduce the concept without overwhelming learners.

Vowels are really important, so be sure to spend plenty of time learning the two sounds that they make. Little learners need to know that all words need vowels because they stick words together.

Short Vowels: ă, ĕ, ĭ, ŏ, ŭ **Long Vowels: ā, ē, ī, ō, ū**
And sometimes *y* that says ē or ī

Set the words below to a tune that you like.
Vowel rap: Point to your child when it is his or her turn to say it:
A says ā.
Repeat after me: ā.
And *a* says ă.
Now you say ă—ă.

E says **ē**.
Repeat after me: **ē**.
E says **ĕ**.
Now you say **ĕ—ĕ**.

I says **ī**.
Repeat after me: **ī**.
And *i* says **ĭ**.
Now you say **ĭ—ĭ**.

O says **ō**.
Repeat after me**:** ō.
And *o* says **ŏ**.
Now you say **ŏ—ŏ**.

U says ū.
Repeat after me: **ū**.
U says **ŭ**.
Now you say **ŭ—ŭ**.

Reading Curriculum in Our Schools
As parents, we can help ensure that our schools are adhering to best practices in literacy that incorporate the science of reading in instruction.

1. Schools need an evidence-based program for all children that includes systematic, explicit, scaffolded instruction in phonics, phonemic awareness, vocabulary, fluency, comprehension, and spelling (e.g., Wilson Foundations, National Geographic Reach). Along with this, they need enhanced teacher training both on the job and in preparatory programs.

2. For struggling readers, schools need intervention programs that include assessments in all five areas of reading that result in targeted goals and progress monitoring. It is critical that this starts in kindergarten when intervention is most successful due to neural plasticity. Parents who have struggling readers should be able to know in which areas their children are struggling and what is being done.

3. Lastly, parents need curriculum transparency in all schools so we know how reading is being taught and how intervention is being done in order for us to support our children's development in partnership with our schools.
Below are articles detailing the current research that necessitates these changes.
https://www.apmreports.org/story/2018/09/10/hard-words-why-american-kids-arent-being-taught-to-read

http://www.edweek.org/ew/articles/2018/10/29/why-doesnt-every-teacher-know-the-research.html

Letters Are Characters!©

Consonant-Vowel-Consonant Words

And E Deserves Special Props

The first words that little readers are ready to tackle after they have broken the phonemic code are three-letter words comprised of a consonant, short vowel, and consonant sounds (for example, *pat*, *pet*, *pit*, *pot*, and *put*). This is a very exciting step for new readers. To do this, explain that when you start to read, you put together the sounds that the letters say—you "sound out" the word. Every letter character gets a turn in order from left to right (show with your finger). Celebrate this accomplishment once your child succeeds. For us, as seasoned readers, it may seem automatic, but for new readers, with new neural pathways, it is magic. During this step, which usually happens at around age six, it is also a great time to review and brush up on phonemic awareness by playing games in which only the first, middle, or last sound of a word is changed. Large letters are always more fun for children.

Here is a game that you can play called the magic wand game.

1. Put the letters c-a-t together. Have your readers sound out the word. Give them plenty of time. Try not to jump in and help them as they work through it unless they get frustrated. They need time to think and process.
2. After they have sounded out the word successfully, cover the letters with a cloth and give your child a magic wand. As they wave their wand, slip your hand under the cloth and change the first letter to *b*. Then pull off the cloth and say, "With a wave of your wand, you turned the *cat* into a *bat*."

You can do this with first, middle, or end sounds.

Phonetic reading blocks are a nice accessory to have during this stage in literacy acquisition.

After the consonant-vowel-consonant skill is solid, you can introduce the concept of brave or magic *e*. A fun way to present this is to talk about *e*'s personality. Review the letter's two sounds (ē and ĕ) with a scared look on your face. Then ask your child if they ever feel braver sticking up for someone other than themselves. Explain that this is the case for *e*. Before *e* sits at the end of the word silently, he tells the little vowel who is saying his short sound between two consonants that he can be brave and say his long sound. The *e* sits quietly at the end of the word and doesn't make a sound. He makes other letters brave by sitting at the end of consonant-vowel-consonant words. Show examples of this and practice.

This rule takes quite a while to become ingrained. Practice it and play with it a lot. Talk about why *e* might want to make other letters feel brave. Try adding *e* to the end of a word using the magic wand game. (Turn *bat* into *bate* or *bit* into *bite*, etc.). E is often children's favorite letter to play with. A character who is frightened and then becomes brave and bold holds a special appeal to little ones who sometimes feel afraid and try to be brave.

Notes:

Teaching letters out of order has advantages, so feel free to use a rational order based on sound if you prefer. Some experts recommend the following order: P, B, T, D, K, G, I, O, F, V, Th, A, S, Z, Sh, U, Ch, J, E, M, N, Ns, Wh, H, L, R, Qu, C, X, and Y. Some little ones think L-M-N-O is one letter because of the alphabet song, so introduction based on sound confusion has merit. But it is also less accessible, so I made the decision to stick with learning the ABCs in order. Now skip around to review sounds and symbols and review similarities and differences!

Additionally, the vowels have complex sounds that they may make in conjunction with other letters such as v and r. At this level of learning, I made the decision to omit these. As your learner progresses, there are tools like Wilson Reading System® "Sound Cards" that are helpful (www.wilsonlanguage.com).

Here's a game to check understanding: Put large letters in a bin. Ask your little one to pull them out and say their sounds. Line them up on the floor and match the babies with the mommies and daddies.

Write the letters with your finger on your child's palm or back and have them tell you which letter you wrote and what sound it makes.

Acknowledgments

There are so many people who helped me along the way by giving encouragement or informing my understanding. Dr. Paul Yellin, founder of the Yellin Center for Mind, Brain, and Education), you are the North Star to so many. Helen Waldren and Diane Lauretano, your guidance was brilliant. Dr. Christine Woodcock (director of reading at American International College), thank you for validating, believing, and helping the project come to life and evolve. Also thank you for adding the fun favorite food dimension to the project. I always appreciate those who are brave enough to encourage an unconventional path; thank you Cyndi Zesk and Dr. Woodside for encouraging me to pursue this idea. Sara Reynolds (certified literacy coach), thank you for fighting so hard to help children, for teaching me and sharing generously, and for being such a force of goodness. To Ann Marie White (director of the Oliver Wolcott Library), thank you for giving me the support that I needed to launch this program and teach a course based on this book at the library and for your deep compassion and spirit of altruism.

Dana Dziedzic, my best friend since age six, I would not have had the confidence to do half of what I have done in my life were it not for your unfaltering support and encouragement. To my other best friends, who always believe in me, laugh with me, see the best in the world, and never give up on their dreams, you know who you are, but I will name you anyway: Cooper Campbell, Annamari Curtiss, Maria Coutant Skinner, Jennifer Jones Persechino, and Jayne Waterfall. And to all of my friends in my hometown of Litchfield, Connecticut who make feel a deep sense of peace and belonging that I treasure and carry with me in all of my endeavors.

And I must acknowledge the Sunflower Girls (you know who you are); you always have celebrated a can-do attitude and live the concept of empowerment. Although we have not worked together as a team in a long time, you continue to inspire me.

Lastly, thank you to my mother and father, sisters, and brother who were/are imaginative and creative and encouraged me to be too.

Thank you to authors and researchers Mark Seidenberg, Sally Shaywitz, Mary Anne Wolf, Louisa Moats, Susan Hall, and Stanislas Dehaene. Your life's work is valued beyond what can be expressed in words. You inform understanding of this essential topic. I have, with great humility, tried to create an application from what I have learned from your work.

Appendix

My book is intended for all children. We learn best how to teach all readers by looking at those who struggle. If you have struggling readers, get them help as early as possible and be sure that they are receiving assessment that pinpoints their area of difficulty and progress monitoring. You should never feel that it is out of your grasp to understand what interventions are being done. Most importantly, don't wait to begin intervention. Start the moment you see a child struggle.

The annotated bibliography contains information on reading in general and information for struggling readers/dyslexic children—95 percent or more of whom can read at an average or better level if they receive the proper interventions.

Resources, Annotated Bibliography, Tips and Techniques

Reading List

Arndt, Elissa J., 2007. "Scientifically Based Reading Programs: What are They and How Do I Know?" Florida Center for Reading Research.
http://www.fcrr.org/science/pdf/arndt/AA_Summer_Institute_July_2007.pdf

*Awes, Alison. 2014. "Supporting the Dyslexic Child in the Montessori Environment." *NAMTA Journal* 39, no. 3: 171–208.

http://www.montessori-namta.org/PDF/FINALSummerJournalPgs.pdf

This article discusses the tools and materials that support a child who learns differently.

Definition: Dyslexia is a specific learning disability that is neurological in origin. It is characterized by difficulties with accurate and/or fluent word recognition and by poor spelling and decoding abilities. These difficulties typically result from a deficit in the phonological component of language that is often unexpected in relation to other cognitive abilities and the provision of effective classroom instruction. Secondary consequences may include problems in reading comprehension and reduced reading experience that can impede the growth of vocabulary and background knowledge (p.175).

The author explains that dyslexic children need systematic multisensory avenues to learn, and this has no correlation to IQ.

Reading disorders affect 15 to 20 percent of the population. The disorder can be mild or severe. *Very important:* Children who read poorly in third grade (age 8 or 9) continue to have reading problems in high school and after. This may indicate that the neural systems become less responsive to intervention as children get older. Children at risk for dyslexia can be identified even before they begin to read.

In addition to the neural systems, reading difficulties diagnosed at age eight or nine are much more difficult to remediate because the initial disadvantage is compounded over time.

"Early diagnosis, joined with effective treatment, can help define the strengths rather than the challenges of the child. Particular attention should be paid to protecting the child's self-concept, as dyslexic children are especially vulnerable to weak self-esteem.

When a child is accused of a lack of motivation, not working to her full ability, being lazy, or not being smart, she begins to doubt herself. These accusations are more common than we might hope because often the potential in the child is clearer than her ability. The child needs the knowledge that she can count on her parents and teachers for unwavering support (p. 181)."

The author notes that *the child's knowledge of letter sounds by age six is the most important indicator of future reading.*

Many dyslexic children compensate with deep imagination, curiosity, and excellent auditory-compensating ability. They often love stories that are read aloud and take great joy in big-picture thinking exercises (there may be a neurological reason for this).

Dyslexia often goes undetected because of lack of teacher training.
Lastly, the article provides details on effective Montessori methods, such as phonemic games, remedial daily lessons, and observation techniques.

"Decoding Before Context" (2018). Literacy How, Empower Teaching Excellence, Vol. 6 no. 18: https://t.e2ma.net/webview/959dgb/6d6d8508e67a71d8f03497d3af755fc5?fbclid=IwAR1_1hUrmnNswuBKC3GvQSa3mJfVuZi-gAPDrEyfxPS5bNhL6Kka44M3oWk (accessed, 2018).

*Dehaene, Stanislas. 2009. *Reading in the Brain*. New York: Viking.
This book details what is known about the neuroscience of reading. It postulates that reading is a relatively modern task and that our neuronal networks are repurposed for reading. It provides details about remediation that is being developed for dyslexia using the latest data.

Chapter six, "The Dyslexic Brain," details findings about the left temporal lobe of dyslexics, providing evidence that there is a neurological reason for otherwise high-functioning individuals to have an impaired ability to read, write, and speak because the phonological processing area is impaired. Also research on the genetics of dyslexia (DYXICQ on chromosome 15, as well as three other genes) is detailed.

The most important thing is how the approach to intervention described. "The brain is a plastic organ which constantly changes and rebuilds itself and for which genes and experience share equal importance. Neuronal migration anomalies, when they are

present, affect only very small parts of the cortex. The child's brain contains millions of redundant circuits that can compensate for each other's deficiencies. Each new learning episode modifies our gene expression patterns and alters our neuronal circuits thus providing the opportunity to overcome dyslexia and other developmental deficiencies. (p. 345)."
Evidence-based interventions can partially restore normal patterns of brain activity in dyslexic children, or alternate pathways can be formed to compensate. The earlier the intervention can be done, the better for both physiological and emotional reasons. Strategies are recommended and detailed.

*Dweck, Carol. 2008. *Mindset, The New Psychology of Success.* New York: Random House.
This book explores the concept of fixed versus growth mind-sets. Individuals with growth mind-sets do not view intelligence as a fixed entity but rather as a construct that is dynamic. It explores how the two mind-sets shape people's thoughts and lives.

*Eide, Brock L., and Fernette F. Eide. 2011. *The Dyslexic Advantage.* New York: Hudson Street Publishing.
This book posits a theory that along with the disorder of dyslexia there are also gifts.

"As we'll describe throughout this book, dyslexic processing also predisposes individuals to important abilities in many mental functions, including:

- three-dimensional spatial reasoning and mechanical ability
- the ability to perceive relationships like analogies, metaphors, paradoxes, similarities, differences, implications, gaps, and imbalances
- the ability to remember important personal experiences and to understand abstract information in terms of specific examples
- the ability to perceive and take advantage of subtle patterns in complex and constantly shifting systems or data sets (p. 18).

The book further explains the history of the discovery of the disorder. (It was discovered in 1896 by British ophthalmologist W. Pringle Morgan, describing a young boy named Percy.) The authors encourage people to think of dyslexia as a learning and processing style as opposed to a disorder.

The authors explain the signs to look for in early detection:

- late talking, leaving out or reversing word parts (*berlapse/relax, wold/world, pasghetti/spaghetti*)

- making up words for things
- inability to rhyme
- inability to break words into phonemes (c-a-t)
- trouble with word retrieval
- slow mastery of tenses, cases, pronouns. and other grammatical rules

Later signs include "problems with handwriting and written expression; basic arithmetic and rote memory for math facts; processing speed; motor coordination; mishearing and difficulty hearing in background noise; visual function for near work; following directions, keeping information in their mind (working memory); mastering procedures; planning and organizing; error detection; time awareness and pacing sequencing; and mental focus and attention (p. 32)"

They posit that it takes dyslexics longer to learn than non-dyslexics. They call this the "square root rule" (page 38).

They also clearly explain explicit learning. "Individuals with procedural learning challenges also typically have difficulty learning simply by observing and imitating others as they perform and complete, complex skill—that is, by *implicit* learning. Instead, they learn better when rules and procedures are broken down into small more easily mastered steps and demonstrated clearly—a process known as explicit learning (p. 36). They divide dyslexic individuals into types: interconnected reasoning, narrative reasoning, dynamic reasoning, and material reasoning.

Flink, David. 2014. *Thinking Differently*. New York: Harper Collins.
Flink, the author, has both dyslexia and ADHD. This book chronicles his journey and gives practical advice to parents of children who learn differently. It also describes his organization, Eye to Eye, which pairs students with learning and attention issues to college students who act as mentors. Three of the most important points of this book are the following:

If a learning difference is suspected, it is advised to get an evaluation as soon as possible because without it, one is not able to advocate effectively for a child. Flink advises choosing the evaluator carefully and gives specific questions to ask. Testing and understanding how your child thinks are the guides to use to put together the pieces of the learning puzzle.
Seeking accommodations is critical to the success of children who learn differently. "Alterations in the way tasks are presented allow children with learning disabilities to complete the same assignments as other students...Alterations in setting, timing,

scheduling, and response type may begin to address some of your child's learning differences. Any reasonable option should be considered as you brainstorm ideas to make learning more accessible for your different thinker."

Tell your story to people who can help and provide support.

Folsome, Jessica Sidler, Knight, Jennifer A., Reed, Deborah K. (2017). "Report of the Kindergarten-Second Grade Phonics Materials Review for the AMES Community School District." Iowa City, IA: Iowa Reading Research Center, University of Iowa. Ames_phonics_curriculum_review_report.pdf

Gillis, Margie. "The Science of Reading: Comprehensive Literacy for ALL Students." Presentation, Haskins Laboratories and Fairfield University, 2017.
http://fl.dyslexiaida.org/wp-content/uploads/sites/33/2017/09/The-Science-of-Reading-by-Margie-Gillis-on-09-23-2017-1.pdf

Grant, Vanessa. "This Could Be What's Behind Your Kid's Problems in School." Today's Parent, February 15, 2018.
https://www.todaysparent.com/toddler/toddler-development/how-retained-primitive-reflexes-could-lead-to-motor-skill-and-behaviour-issues/
(accessed, 2019).

Hall, Susan L., and Louisa C. Moats, EdD. 1999. *Straight Talk about Reading*. Chicago: Contemporary Books.
This book is written for parents who want to teach their children to read. It provides helpful information and practical tips. It also covers in detail why reading instruction is not science based.

Hanford, Emily. 2018. "Hard Words: Why Aren't Our Kids Being Taught to Read?" APMreports.
https://www.apmreports.org/story/2018/09/10/hard-words-why-american-kids-arent-being-taught-to-read

Hanford, Emily. "Why Are We Still Teaching Reading the Wrong Way?" New York Times, October 26, 2018.
https://www.nytimes.com/2018/10/26/opinion/sunday/phonics-teaching-reading-wrong-way.html

Hessler, Terri. (2017). "Why is Structured Literacy Missing From So Many Teacher Programs." International Dyslexia Association.
https://dyslexiaida.org/why-is-structured-literacy-missing-from-so-many-teacher-programs/ (accessed 2019).

"How Structured Literacy Saved My Children." Boulder Valley Kids Identified with Dyslexia.
https://www.bvkid.org/2018/07/03/how-structured-literacy-saved-my-children/ (accessed 2018).

Morey, Anne-Marie. "What Tigers Can Teach Us About Letter Reversals." Bay Tree Blog.
http://www.baytreelearning.com/blog/2014/06/16/letter-reversals/
(accessed 2018).

Pimentel, Susan. (2018). "Why Doesn't Every Teacher Know the Research on Reading Instruction." Education Week, January 4, 2018.
http://www.edweek.org/ew/articles/2018/10/29/why-doesnt-every-teacher-know-the-research.html

Rathbun, Guy. "Audio Story: Language at the Speed of Sight." PRX.
https://beta.prx.org/stories/195742 (accessed, 2019).

Rello and Baeza-Yates. 2013. Good Fonts for Dyslexia. Washington: Assets.
http://dyslexiahelp.umich.edu/sites/default/files/good_fonts_for_dyslexia_study.pdf

Satullo, Sara, K. "Bethelehem Kindergartners Make Stunning Strides in Reading." Lehighvalleylive.com
https://www.lehighvalleylive.com/bethlehem/index.ssf/2017/06/bethlehem_kindergartners_makin.html (accessed, 2019).

Shaywitz, Sally. 2005. *Overcoming Dyslexia*. New York: First Vintage Books.
http://dyslexia.yale.edu/book_Overcoming.html
This is an extremely important book for any struggling reader.

Seidenberg, Mark. 2017. *Language at the Speed of Sight.* New York: Basic Books.
This book is a must read for anyone who wants to understand fully the evolution of reading and why the science of reading isn't used to construct reading curriculum in the United States.

The book explicates reading disorders/dyslexia explaining that this developmental disorder is on a continuum and the response to intervention is an appropriate measure to use for treatment. Since we cannot "look under the hood to see the brain" we must rely on behavioral evidence, genetic factors and factor in protective elements to determine needs.

Torgensen, Joseph, K. (2004). "Avoiding the Devastating Downward Spiral." American Federation of Teachers, ALF-CIO, (Accessed, 2018).
https://www.aft.org/periodical/american-educator/fall-2004/avoiding-devastating-downward-spiral

Tyre, Peg. "Yes, There's a Right Way to Teach Reading." Great Schools.org, November 26, 2018.
https://www.greatschools.org/gk/articles/importance-of-reading-success/
(accessed, 2018).

Wolf, Maryanne. 2008. *The Story and Science of the Reading Brain.* New York: Harper.
This book presents an important perspective on what reading does for us, how it shapes and changes our minds, thoughts, and brains. The exploration of reading as an occasion with the self that is both generative and transformative is illuminating. The last third of the book presents a comprehensive look at reading disorders/dyslexia. The section first explores the damage that is done to children because educators are often ill-equipped to help them.

"You will never understand what it feels like to be dyslexic. No matter how long you have worked in this area, no matter if your own children are dyslexic, you will never understand what it feels like to be humiliated your entire childhood and taught every day to believe that you will never succeed at anything (p. 165)." (Quote from Jackie Stewart, Scottish race car driver.)

"Children with any form of dyslexia are not 'dumb' or 'stubborn': nor are they 'not working to potential'—the three most frequent descriptions they endure. However, they will be mistakenly described in these ways many times by many people, including themselves. It is vital for parents and teachers to work to ensure that all children with any form of reading problem receive immediate, intensive intervention and that no child or adult equates reading problems with low intelligence. A comprehensive support system should be in place from the first indication of difficulty until the child becomes an independent, fluent reader, or the frustrations of reading failure can lead to a cycle of learning failure, dropping out and delinquency. Most important the considerable potential of these children will be lost to themselves and to society (p. 194)." Wolf stresses the fact that we know how to teach these children, and it is our failure if we don't. Rapid automatized naming (RAN) tests are discussed as an effective way to identify those who my be struggling readers even before they begin to read (see pages 283–285).

Torgesen, Joseph, K. 2004. "Avoiding the Devastating Downward Spiral: The Evidence that Early Intervention Prevents Reading Failure." 2004. *American Educator*, Fall. https://www.aft.org/periodical/american-educator/fall-2004/avoiding-devastating-downward-spiral.

Wasik, Barbara, A. (2001). "Phonemic Awareness and Young Children." Childhood Education, 77 3: 128-133. http://www.sevenhillscharter.org/docs/phonemicawarenessarticles/paphonemicawarenessandyoungchildren.pdf

Wolf, Maryanne. 2018. *Reader, Come Home: The Reading Brain in the Digital World.* New York: HarperCollins

Useful Websites and PDFs

http://community.dyslexicadvantage.org/
http://www.proactiveparent.com/
http://readingmatterstomaine.org/
http://dyslexia.yale.edu/PAR_EarlyIntervention.html

Partial List of Teaching Resources

Adams, Marilyn Jager, Barbara R. Foorman, Ingvar Lundberg, and Terri Beller. 2014. *Phonemic Awareness in Young Children.* Baltimore: Paul H. Brookes Publishing Co.

Bell, Nanci. 1997. *Seeing Stars.* California, Gander Press.

The Bob books: http://bobbooks.com/

Earobics Step 1, Home Version: Sound Foundations for Reading & Spelling. 1997. Houghton Mifflin (available on Amazon).

Handwriting without Tears: https://www.lwtears.com/hwt

High-frequency words: http://www.k12reader.com/dolch-word-list/

Orlassino, Cheryl. 2014. *I Can Read, Book A: Orton-Gillingham Based Reading Lessons for Young Students Who Struggle with Reading and May Have Dyslexia:* New York: Creative Dragon Press

Learning with Homer (app)
One More Story (app)

Partial List of Effective Multisensory Techniques

For Symbol Imagery

Finger painting words
Letter matching game – match parents to baby letters
Magic wand game—see page 87
Magnetic board writing
Tracing Letters on sensory bags
Shaving cream painting wring with fingers
Wet/Dry/Try with a blackboard
Whisper game
Writing the letter with your finger on child's hand or back and having them identify the letter
Writing in the dark with a tiny flashlight

Other Teaching Techniques

Three period lesson—https://www.montessoriservices.com/ideas-insights/the-three-period-lesson

(photo credit)
Terry Augustyn, Nutmeg Photography

Caroline Wilcox Ugurlu, pictured with Daisy, who was not helpful during the writing of this book because she enjoys walking on keyboards. She is, however, a good reading partner for adults and children alike.

"*Letters Are Characters* is a creative, fun, and imaginative way for kids to learn their letters. When my son made his letters, they were his own, and he remembered them. Books, videos, and magnets added little value to his learning, but building them and connecting letters to personalities made a huge difference in his learning on his path to phonetic awareness and reading."

—Tyler Stevens

"Ms. Wilcox Ugurlu has made the science of early reading instruction - which IS rocket science – accessible to everyone. This parent-friendly program presents the current research about early reading acquisition and provides step-by-step instructions for supporting any young child's literacy development. The Letters are Characters activities are engaging and play-like, while incorporating research-based methods. A wonderful resource for parents!"

—Sara Reynolds, Elementary Reading Specialist, Torrington School District

CPSIA information can be obtained
at www.ICGtesting.com
Printed in the USA
BVHW021025150419
545535BV00022B/1581/P